BRIGHT LIGHTS
DARK SKIES

JESS HANNA

ISBN: 978-1-954771-14-7

Cover Design: Jakki Jelene

Published in the United States of America

To those who feel lost. There is one who knows
how to find you, even in the darkest of nights.

ACKNOWLEDGMENTS

First and always, I have to thank my lord and savior, Jesus Christ, for granting me the privilege of writing this and many other strange stories.

Jakki, your encouragement, support, and criticism has been invaluable in making this book happen. Without your involvement and spark of inspiration this story may have never been written. Thank you for allowing me to exploit your fears.

Last, but never least, I would like to thank you, the reader. Without you, all of this would be in vain.

A man that flees from his fear may find that he has only taken a shortcut to meet it.

—JRR Tolkien

• INTRODUCTION •

I never thought I would believe that UFOs, space aliens, extraterrestrials, little green men, little grey men, alien abduction, or close encounters of any kind actually existed. What rational person would? And yet I can't deny the truth of what I have seen with my own eyes and felt in my own flesh. The things I experienced defy any other natural explanation, including anything psychological. I wish I had some psychosis that could explain it all way, but I have no diagnosed mental disease and was not a part of any mass hypnosis. I have also experienced no form of sleep paralysis in the medical sense.

Several hundred thousand Unidentified Flying Objects have been spotted by a variety of people in nearly all areas of the world over the years. The number of people who have reported being abducted numbers in the millions, with more being added to that total every day. It seems clear even to a know-nothing schlub like me that something is happening here. But what?

I can't see your face, but I have a good idea what you are thinking. If you are like me, I thought the same thing at one time. You don't believe me. And who would? But don't worry. My story is as much for you as it is for those who believe in those mysterious life forms living among the stars with their whole hearts. Humans are, after all, incredibly arrogant to assume to be the only intelligent beings in the universe, right?

The answers to those questions given by the so-called experts can seem vague at best, and evasive at worst. The very idea of the existence of life outside of Earth suggests the possibility that there may not be a God who created it all, chaos reigns supreme, and we are all here by randomness and chance; descendants of the primordial ooze, destined to live and die...for nothing.

And if these creatures from beyond our galaxy exist, what is their purpose? Who are these superior beings that seem preoccupied with appearing to earthlings for no reason, abducting and examining them, and in some cases having sexual encounters with humans for no apparent purpose? What is it that drives them or draws them to us? Is there something in humans that is special, or are we just another stop in their interstellar studies of the various galaxies throughout the endless expanse of space?

I have written this book to share my experience and the information I learned on my quest for the truth. I have no doubt that I can convince you that UFOs and aliens exist. They are real and they are among us. The real question is what are they, and what is their purpose?

Since this is my story, it will be heavily slanted in favor of my findings. I am not setting out to be purely objective, but to share what I have gone through, along with my thoughts, fears, failures, and victories along the way. Feel free to scoff at me if you must. I expect it.

I make what I feel are some startling claims about the intentions of these visitors. And while I cannot prove anything using empirical methods, I can offer my eyewitness testimony and hope that anyone reading this will keep an open mind and not judge me too harshly until the end. The end of what? The end of this book, or the end of all things, whichever comes first.

SIGHTINGS

• 1 •

When it all started, I worked the second shift as a security guard at the Avondale Farms fruit processing plant. I was one of six guards charged with keeping watch on the factory and the surrounding property. Most of the time I sat in a small lighted booth situated at the front gate. During the day it was left open to allow factory employees, visitors, and deliveries of damaged fruit and vegetables that local farms were unable to sell as whole produce. These rejects were ground into pulp and turned into juices, applesauce, baby carrots, and a variety of other processed plant-based food items that I generally avoided. Not because I am a health nut. I just hate the taste of most fruits and vegetables. And I know how these foods are made. But that's a less important story for another time.

The second shift ran from three in the afternoon to midnight, with an hour break to eat what passed for lunch at that time in my life. Most days I ate some kind of processed meat on white bread with a side of chips. I was supposed to have a partner to share the responsibility of walking the perimeter to make sure the building was intact and secure. On that particular night, I was alone. The other guard – I can't remember his name – was scheduled for the second shift, but had called in sick. And there was no one else that could fill in for him. I was okay with it. If I had my way I would have worked alone every day.

I had just returned from walking the perimeter at what should have been the end of my shift. I rubbed my hands together to warm them. The nights were still cold, despite the fact that the late spring sun warmed the days.

I unlocked the door to the booth, stepped inside, and locked it behind me. The small space heater I'd bought with my own money did a pretty good job of heating up the space. I sat in a ratty castaway office chair and held my hands over the heat emanating from the portable unit.

I looked at my watch. It was five past midnight and my relief was nowhere in sight. John was late more often than he was on time. Alicia was no better. Both of them were full of all kinds of excuses.

John worked another job during the day and had trouble waking up two hours after he'd fallen asleep. Alicia had three kids at home and couldn't leave the house until her husband came home from his afternoon shift at the plastics plant. I sat back in the chair and sighed. It would have been nice if they came to work on time. I wanted to go home.

The phone in the security booth rang, startling me. I let it ring a second time before picking it up. "Avondale Farms. This is Alex. How can I help you?"

"Hi, Alex. It's John. I overslept again. I'm sorry for being late and will get there as soon as I can."

Of course.

I inhaled deeply and pushed the air out through my nose, closing my eyes in an attempt to diffuse the annoyance I felt. Instead of telling him what I really thought, I just said, "It's okay, John. Just get here when you can."

He thanked me and hung up. I could tell he felt bad for being late, and I couldn't really blame him. He was trying to support his family, working two full-time jobs that did not equal the pay of the one full-time job he hoped to get after attending classes online.

The phone rang again.

"Avondale Farms. This is Alex. How can I help you?"

"Alex, it's Alicia. Little Tommy is throwing up all over the place. I'm not going to be able to come in tonight. Is John there yet?"

I leaned my head back in the chair and closed my eyes. If I wasn't so aggravated, I might have laughed. "No worries, Alicia. John's not here yet. He called and said he's on his way. Just take care of Tommy. I hope he feels better."

She thanked me just as profusely as John did. I returned the phone to the cradle and looked around the booth. The checklist that Prime Security insisted we complete for each shift hung on a nail next to the door. I pulled the clipboard off the wall and mindlessly checked off all the tasks. Most I had completed, and the ones I hadn't didn't matter anyway. No one was going to double check my work, and there was nothing at the factory to guard against anyway. The remote location, high fence and the presence of twenty-four-hour security kept away any vandals. There was no money kept on site, and no one in their right mind would want to steal fruits and vegetables that were deformed or near to inedible without all the crushing, squeezing, and pulverizing that they required.

Most of the time when I did the perimeter checks I saw nothing. Some nights brought scavengers like raccoons, coyotes, or an occasional deer. Once I saw a bear, but I have never seen anything warranting the level of security Avondale Farms required. Much of the reason my job existed was due to the fact that the property was fifteen miles from the very edge of suburban civilization. Avondale Farms itself sat about five miles closer to town and was where most of the more urban-minded folks went to experience a day in the country during the harvest season. No one came out to tour the plant.

When I looked at my watch again forty-five minutes had passed. I looked out the window of the booth, straining to see the familiar shine of headlights coming toward me. There was nothing but darkness in the distance both ways. I sat back down and realized that it was time to take another walk around the fence and building. I almost decided to skip it and simply mark it off the list. I sometimes wish I had done just that.

When I was about to stand up, the overhead fluorescent lights in the booth flickered and buzzed. As I lifted my head I saw a fast moving orange or pink light rush by in the strip of sky just above the tree line that was visible from the window of the security booth. I stood up fast from my seat and opened the door to try to catch sight of the strange lights before they faded into the night. A faint trail that could very well have been the afterglow of the white light burning at the back of my eyes from staring at the fluorescent lights streaked across my field of vision. I walked down a couple of steps.

I blinked and rubbed my eyes, looking again. The

sky was clear. There were no more orange or pink streaks. From the bottom step, I looked behind me at the booth and the lights inside had stopped their epileptic fit. It was probably nothing more than shoddy workmanship by some drunken electrician who figured his work was good enough.

I rushed back inside the booth, snatched my key ring off the hook, then locked and slammed the door behind me. I decided to go ahead and make a final sweep of the factory grounds. The walk was almost always the same. Scrub oaks, pine, and maple trees surrounded the property. They had just started sprouting new leaves and a light wind rustled them. The forest in that part of the county was deep and mostly undisturbed. I never considered myself an easily spooked person, but I rarely pointed the flashlight anywhere but straight ahead, especially on nights when I worked alone. I had no reason to go looking for trouble.

My hope was that John would be there to meet me when I returned. I was disappointed but not surprised to find that he was not there. It was turning into the kind of night where I'd end up working twelve hours instead of eight. I unlocked the door to the guard shack and stepped inside. I checked the phone to see if there were any waiting messages. If there were any, a bright red light would shine as bright as Rudolph's nose. The phone was dark.

At quarter to two, I prepared myself mentally to make another short trip around the building. I thought about skipping it again, but decided I should do at least that much if I was unwilling to do every little thing suggested on the silly checklist. I rose from the chair and let a curse slip out as I snatched the flashlight from the desk. No one was around to hear me at that hour anyway, so what difference did it really make how I talked to myself?

I stepped outside and had just finished locking the door when I heard the sound of an approaching vehicle. I stepped to the side of the booth so that I could get a good view of the road. Two headlights appeared as a vehicle crested a small hill in the distance. As the lights grew brighter, I became convinced that it was not John, but some other blue collar hero on the way home from a late shift at another factory, hospital, or security gig.

I waited by the side of the booth as the twin lights drew closer and slowed. A mid-sized sedan pulled up beneath the arc-sodium lights lining the entrance to the facility. I instinctively unlatched the holster attached to my belt and prepared to draw my revolver. The car stopped near the little gate to the side of the larger sliding gate. A car door opened.

John stepped out of the passenger side, looking disheveled. His jacket was torn and dirty and his blue dress shirt hung out of the bottom of one side. I heard him talking to the driver, but could not make out the specific words. He appeared apologetic and thankful at the same time, his usual look in those days. After a few more words to the unseen driver, he shut the door with a solid thunk. The car reversed, shifted into drive, and drove back the way it had come. I watched the red tail lights fade into the night until they disappeared past the small hill.

As John approached, I walked toward him and fought the urge to roll my eyes. He gave me an awkward smile before he fished his keys out of his pocket, unlocked the smaller gate and stepped inside. He gave me the same sorry look he'd given the unseen driver of the car. It would be easier to be mad at him if I didn't know that he was sincere. Some people have all the bad luck.

"Alex, I am so sorry. My car broke down again and I had to walk back to my brother's house to ask for a ride to work. I feel terrible for making you wait." He lifted his cap with the Prime Security logo emblazoned across the front panel and raked his hand through his buzzed blond hair before planting the cap back into place.

"It's okay, John. Really. I wish you could have called me, but I understand. Things happen." *They seemed to happen to John and Alicia all the time and to me almost never*, I thought but did not say.

"Thanks, Buddy. I owe you one." He clapped me on the shoulder in a gesture of goodwill.

He owed me much more than just the one he claimed to owe me at that moment. Instead of calling him out and demanding payment for all the ones he owed me, I smiled back and let it slide. "No worries, John. Seriously."

He gave me an aw-shucks grin. "Thanks a lot, man. You really saved my butt today. I appreciate you covering for me."

"It's what I do." I turned and walked back to the booth to put the flashlight back on the desk. It was time to go home.

After I'd walked through the little gate and waved goodbye to John, I climbed into my beat up Ford box truck. It was older than it had any right to be and always seemed to be on its last leg. Somehow it managed to keep chugging along, despite being well past its prime in years and mileage. John often joked that it would just disintegrate one day and I'd be left standing in a pile of rust and bolts. There was more than a nugget of truth in that statement. I thought about his words as I started the engine and put it in reverse. I smirked as I recalled that my vehicle was not the one that had broken down that night.

● ● ●

The way home was a twenty-mile drive further into the wilderness to the tiny village of Big River. The single gas station, bar, and greasy spoon that constituted the center of town never lived up to its namesake. It was so small that it didn't even warrant a single flashing red light at the one four-way stop. Big River was cursed with being in between the way back and the road to nowhere. No one ever stopped long enough to pay it much attention.

I'd inherited the house I grew up in when my parents passed, along with the eighty acres they'd intended to make into a farm. It was a dream that never happened. At the beginning of their lives together, my mother struggled to have children. In time, she managed to crank out me and my little sister Lily. It had been months or possibly years since Lily had checked in to let me know how she was getting on. I hoped she was having the better life she dreamed of when she was growing up.

I was making good time on the drive home with no traffic in either direction. I'd left the window cracked to allow some of the cool night air to circulate through the cabin. It was brisk and refreshing. The radio in the truck had long since died and went without being replaced, and the rush of cool air on my face kept me alert as I scanned the road for deer or any other animals that might get the idea into their heads to cross the road.

The pale yellow headlights of the truck illuminated the tree line at the edges of both sides of the lonely, familiar road. I could have driven the route with my eyes closed, but more than one poor deer had met their demise with the last thing they ever saw being the dull chrome grill of my truck. They barely left a dent in the old beast.

I was just over halfway home when the truck started chugging and hitching like it was going to stall. It had never sputtered at any point in past, not even on the coldest of mornings, so this was odd behavior. I tramped the gas pedal in an attempt to flood the engine, maybe clear out the carburetor. The truck continued to struggle down the road but did not die.

"Come on girl. At least make it home."

I'd driven another mile when everything in the truck just quit. There were no idiot lights to warn me that anything was wrong. Everything just stopped working. The headlights went out. The engine was dead. I used what remaining forward motion I had to coast to the shoulder and eased as far onto the dirt as I could without slipping into the ditch with the half-light of the moon as my guide.

Acting on instinct, I pulled the switch to turn on the hazard lights. Nothing happened, of course, and I was confused for a second before realizing my stupidity. I turned the key back into the off position in the ignition and sat for a few seconds, considering my options. I was ten miles from home, ten miles from work, and twenty-five miles from the nearest moderately populated city. In short, I was stranded.

I unbuckled my seatbelt and turned around to climb onto the seat bench and reach behind it to retrieve my roadside emergency kit. It was one I put together myself with jumper cables, flares, a flashlight, a hammer, a couple of screwdrivers, a small first aid kit, and one of those reflective blankets.

I pulled the kit out from behind the seat, turned around to face forward, unzipped the thick canvas bag, and pulled out the flashlight. It was a cheap plastic one that I had bought at a dollar store for just this purpose. I turned it in my hands, found the switch, and moved it into the on position. Nothing happened. I smacked it against my other hand and tried again. Still nothing.

Frustrated, I unscrewed the top and confirmed that it had batteries. I already knew it did. I was meticulous about making sure my roadside emergency kit was well stocked and refreshed every six months. After all, the eventual demise of my battered truck could have come at any time. In a vain attempt to deny the deadness of the flashlight, I rearranged the order of the batteries, screwed the top back on, and flipped the switch again. Nothing.

I tossed the flashlight back into the bag and reached for a flare. I had one in my hand when the radio blared to life, spewing loud static. I froze in place, not registering what was happening. The face of the radio flickered with low yellow light. The static grew louder and ebbed and flowed, the sound oscillating back and forth between the speakers I thought were dead. No sound had come out of them for years. I dropped the unlit flare and reached to lock the driver side door, then leaned over and locked the passenger door. I swallowed a hard lump in my throat.

The static was infused with a high pitched whine that traveled across the audio field in a well-defined wave pattern. I could almost see a bump of water moving across the ocean toward the shore in my mind. The one thing I knew about waves was that they crested and broke.

The first flutters of anxiety attacked my stomach. I breathed faster as my eyes darted back and forth into the darkness, but there was nothing to see but trees and road. The radio grew louder, more insistent.

I had no plan, no idea about what I should do, so I did nothing. I sat behind the steering wheel and looked out the windshield. I turned my head left and right to look out the side windows as well as the window behind me. Something inexplicable was happening. The only piece of technology (if you could still call it that) that was working in my decrepit truck was something that hadn't worked in years. True, the light coming from the face of the radio was low, but it was present. And it should not have been.

I was like a furtive animal, acting on instinct. And my instinct was to hide. The wave of static coming from the should-be-dead speakers became more pronounced. My heart responded by beating a little faster. A creeping feeling tickled my spine, persistent in a way that made me feel vulnerable. Having no experience with the supernatural, unnatural, strange, or bizarre, I wasn't sure what horrors awaited me. I didn't have to wait too long to find out.

The radio screeched and made a popping sound as it went dead. My ears rang with the absence of sound. The light of the half moon once again became the sole source of illumination in the cab of the truck. I reached into the bag for another flare, preparing myself to get out of the truck. There was no way I could stay locked in there all night. It was a long time until morning, and if the past ten minutes were any indication of coming events, I had no desire to stick around to see what happened next.

As I reached for the door handle a bright white light from above the truck filled the cabin and blinded me. My first thought was that it was a police helicopter like the ones I'd seen on TV chasing down criminals. But I'd never seen one out in the sticks. There was no need for that sort of equipment with so few people. We were lucky if the Forest County Sheriff's Department could spare a deputy or two to do a drive by once or twice a week in a Crown Vic or an SUV that was nearly as old as my dilapidated truck.

I pulled my hand back from the door handle and pushed myself into the center of the bench seat. The light moved slowly from the driver's side to the passenger side, then winked out. I was blinded again as my eyes adjusted to the darkness. All I could see for a few seconds were shadows. I reached for the roadside emergency kit.

I dropped the flare I still held in my hand as the light blazed bright once again. It seemed to be focused above the center of the truck cabin. I sat still, my eyes wide with fear. My stomach growled and I felt my bowels loosen. It was a bad time to have the sudden urge to take a crap. I leaned forward and tried to look up into the light. It was too bright, too strong for my eyes.

The spotlight winked out again, but I was not plunged into blindness or darkness. Instead, I saw a pattern of spinning lights reflected off the windshield. Orange, pink, and green swirled across the hood. I felt and heard a low humming, similar to the sensation of strong bass at a rock concert or from a tricked out car, but this was different. There was no thumping beat, just a steady low vibration that grew stronger with each passing second. The windows started to rattle in their tracks.

I decided to make a break for it. I didn't know how to go about doing that sort of thing, but I'd seen enough movies to know that if the backcountry hick stays in his car in the middle of the woods while otherworldly things happen, he is bound to get kidnapped, killed, or both. Fighting my instinct to stay, I grabbed one of the flares I dropped on the floor, scooted back across the seat to the driver's side, opened the door, and slid to the ground. Dust kicked back into my face.

The humming was more intense outside the truck and louder. With my face to the ground, I scooched myself under the truck. My shining moment bravery that prompted me to get out of the truck was gone, and I was again a frightened little rabbit hiding from the crafty fox. The lights flickered all around me. Orange, pink, and green rotated in a clockwise circle.

I was seized by the sudden urge to see the source of the lights, to confirm that it was more than my imagination. I cursed myself for my curiosity, knowing there was no way I could resist the urge to look. I rolled over onto my back and stared at the undercarriage of the truck for a few moments in an attempt to distract myself. My truck wasn't one of those new low riders, so there was plenty of ground clearance underneath. I'd never needed any car jacks to do any repairs. Everything was rusty, but there were no leaks.

Taking a deep breath to steel myself, I scooted over toward the driver side, closer to the road. I positioned myself so that my head was the only thing that would stick out from the side of the truck. I figured that a smaller target would be harder to hit. Common sense told me to get back under the truck.

Unable to resist the magnetism of curiosity, I pulled myself by the frame of the truck until half of my head stuck out from the side. I kept my eyes closed until I saw the lights dancing on the back of my eyelids. I wasn't ready to look. At least not yet. If I could just keep my eyes closed, I wouldn't have to see whatever was out there to see. I found myself wishing I'd been born blind.

Disgusted by my cowardice, I gripped the side of the truck as hard as I could and forced my eyes open as wide as possible. What I saw took my breath away. Probably a hundred feet up in the air, a large disc hovered over the road, nearly silent except for the low-frequency hum I heard and felt deep in the marrow of my bones. The orange, pink, and green lights spun around the outside of the structure. Another set of softer white lights spun counterclockwise inside the colorful circle.

I was struck by the realization that the hum was the only sound I heard. The crickets, frogs, and other insects that were born like crazy in late spring were silent. They should have filled the night with their chaotic symphony. I strained to hear anything else aside from the low hum as I gazed into the dazzling display of lights. The silver colored metal I could see on the bottom of the craft gleamed dully with reflected glory. It was mesmerizing.

Scrounging up a bit more courage and casting ideas of self-preservation aside, I pulled myself out from under the truck and stumbled to my feet. I pressed my back into the driver side door, relieved to find it was still there and felt solid. It was real. My left hand brushed a piece of exposed rust on the body. I clutched it in my hand to keep my tenuous grip on reality firm. I closed my eyes and held tightly to those things within my immediate grasp. To think of anything else was too much for my mind to comprehend. It must have looked like I was performing some form of worship, stricken by a hypnotic spirit and staring into the face of my god.

I couldn't bring myself to say the word spaceship

or UFO, but that was exactly what hovered above me. My self-denial was always strong, and never more so that in the face of unknown situations. I wondered how long the object would stay suspended above my truck and part of me wanted to know what it was doing there. Why did it seem to be making me the focus of its attention? There was nothing special about me, nothing extraordinary.

I felt the hum grow weaker before I heard its volume drop. I snapped open my eyes and watched as a bright streak of light flamed out across the night sky. It looked like a shooting star or a meteorite, except without the long tail. It didn't take long for the ball of light to disappear completely. I stayed glued to the side of the truck, staring into the sky, entranced by the spell of the special kind of magic I'd just experienced. I exhaled for what felt like the first time in hours.

My eyes adjusted to the darkness, searching the shadows for some sort of explanation for what I had just seen. There was no physical evidence left behind that I could hold onto. There was nothing more than my experience of a metal disc in the sky and some spinning lights. And I couldn't forget the low hum that penetrated through the core of my being and punched a hole in my soul. There was no other way to describe it.

I realized my right hand was still clutched around the flare when I turned to open the door to the truck. I moved it to my left hand and wrenched the door open. As I climbed in, I tossed the flare toward the direction of my makeshift roadside emergency kit on the bench seat. I reached in the dark for the flashlight. I grabbed it by the light end, turned it in my hand, and flicked the switch. Light so bright it made me wince filled the cabin. A feeling of tightness poked at my chest. I suddenly found it hard to breathe. And then I started shaking.

Desperate to regain control of the fragile tension in my own little world, I fumbled the key one notch forward in the ignition. The dashboard and headlights lit up, strong as ever. Air pumped out from the heater fan. I pressed the clutch to the floor and twisted the key further to start the engine. The truck roared to life. I shifted the car into neutral and pressed down on the brake. My body trembled harder and my pulse became erratic. It didn't race. It skipped. It leapt. It jumped in its own kind of sporadic rhythm. My mouth felt dry, filled with an uncomfortable cottony sensation.

There was one more test of my sanity left. I reached over to the radio that suddenly came to life when everything else that had previously worked went dead. I pushed the power button on and waited for the wave-like static. Nothing happened.

That was all my mind could take. A rush of emotion that can only be described as complete unrelief coursed through my veins and I cried my first tears of fear and confusion. It was a dangerous mix of paralyzing emotion that came unbidden and seemed too terrible to bear. And it would not be the worst or even the last time I felt such a thing.

• 2 •

With the truck idling in neutral and my foot on the brake, I buried my face in my hands and wept. Of course, the tears stopped after a time. But it was a long time. So long, in fact, that I have no idea how long it really was. The passage of time seemed irrelevant, just one long stream of indeterminate seconds. My memories of that breakdown were like a series of flashes from a camera, all still shots and no motion. And yet that time of emotional release and reflection revealed nothing that made any sense of the situation.

Once I was able to see through the blur of my tears, I put the truck into gear and started on my way home. The gravel on the side of the road spit out from under the rear tires. The rubber squeaked sharply as they grabbed hold of the pavement. Like an old man on the verge of losing his driver's license, I drove much slower than I should have, leaning forward as far as I could in an effort to see as much of the road in the darkness as possible.

My eyes felt stretched and puffy from crying. I knew they were probably bloodshot, and if I was pulled over by the Forest County Sheriff's Department I would have a hard time explaining myself. I'd most likely be hauled in for suspected drug use with my swollen red eyes, trembling body, and overall frazzled demeanor. Catching a quick glance of myself in the mirror, I confirmed I looked just as bad as I felt.

As I continued to drive, the shifting shadows on either side of the road made me more tense. Shapes appeared and disappeared in the swirling darkness, a product of dewy mist that rose from the forest floor and my over-stimulated imagination. Safety reflectors that marked the edge of the road became eyes of unknown beasts, waiting to pounce out of the darkness as the truck chugged forward.

I thought I saw the dull reflection of deer eyes on the passenger side of the road about a hundred yards ahead. I confirmed this fact as I let my foot off the gas and coasted by a small group of the meek animals huddled against the tree line. Their heads turned to follow me as I passed. They were not the healthy, fat deer I'd dodged driving down this road my whole life. The brown and white creatures looked emaciated from the long winter and cold spring. Their coats were grimy and matted. I wondered if they had caught some sort of disease.

The stretch of road ahead of me that I'd traveled countless times became a place I no longer recognized. It had been invaded by that thing with the spinning lights. Everything from the faded white lines that marked the two-lane road to the forest that created a canopied tunnel and the animals that lived beyond the trees was off balance, threatening somehow. I wanted nothing more than to be transported home into my warm bed with my trusty German Shepherd Charlie asleep on the floor. The remaining miles stretched further than seemed possible. And then I saw a light of hope.

As I rounded a big curve, my farmhouse came into view. Most of the large structure was hidden in shadows, but the lights on either side of the front door, hidden under the roof of the front porch, shone like torches, beckoning me to familiar comforts. The lights illuminated a small portion of the front yard. The pedestal lamp I left on in the living room made the front picture window glow, creating the illusion of occupancy while I was at work. And if that wasn't enough to deter potential burglars, anyone who dared approach the house with plans of breaking in would be welcomed by Charlie. His large canine teeth, intimidating snarl, and powerful bark made for an impressive deterrent.

My mind worked overtime, enhancing all of my five senses. As I turned onto the gravel driveway I felt and heard the stones crunch underneath the tires. I took my time driving up to the garage that was attached to the house by a breezeway my father had built ages ago. The motion sensor spotlights on either side of the garage lit up as I approached. I looked to the left and the two-story whitewashed farmhouse I'd lived in for my whole life felt different. Shadows lurked around every corner of the surrounding yard not penetrated by the lights inside the house and on the garage. I pressed the button on the remote to open the garage door. It creaked loudly as the metal door rolled up into its track. Once it stopped moving I drove inside.

I sat in the truck, not wanting to get out, but knowing that Charlie would want to see me. He was probably pacing back and forth at the inside door on the house side of the breezeway, anticipating my arrival. I'd meant to get another pet to keep him company when I first brought him home but had never gotten around to it. Then ten years passed, and it didn't seem fair to bring in someone else to split my attention.

Charlie wasn't trapped in the house though. Knowing I would be gone for long hours at work, I installed a flapping doggy door on the back side of the house that let out into a fenced off portion of the backyard. The lawn was well worn or bare in that section, evidence of the time he spent there.

When I was home and could easily observe my overgrown puppy dog, I let him roam free. The closest neighbors were about two miles away with nothing but fields of untended land and wilderness between us and them.

My typical routine when I came home from work was to get out of the truck, close the garage door using the button on the panel next to the door leading to the breezeway, then work my way to the house. That night was anything but routine. I could not get the spinning lights of the disc-shaped thing I saw levitating a hundred feet above my truck out of my mind. I looked in the rearview mirror, not knowing what I expected to see, but relieved all the same that there was nothing but the dimly lit yard in the reflection.

Before exiting the truck I used the remote to close the garage door instead of getting out first. The sectioned metal roared to life and rolled back down the track with its tortured squeak. Once I heard it clamp down behind me, I felt safe enough to exit. I reached toward the ignition to turn off the engine and noticed my hand was shaking again. Or shaking still. I wasn't sure which. I turned the key back and pulled it out. The key ring jangled in my trembling hand.

I opened the truck door with my left hand and pushed it wide open. It squealed as it swung out. Between that noise and the squeaking of the garage door, I had another two chores to add to my ever-growing list. I remained planted in the driver's seat, unable to stop my mind from exploring what I'd seen earlier. Determined to not allow myself to be frozen in fear, I stepped out and shut the door. It squeaked on its way back before closing with a solid thump. I thought again about getting a new truck. Anything to distract myself.

As I walked through the breezeway, I heard Charlie scratching at the house door on the other end. I could almost see his happy face, his backside wagging his tail, instead of the other way around. I smiled as I thought about my constant companion; the one friend who would never leave me.

As soon as I approached the threshold, the scratching stopped. He could sense my presence on the other side. I knew he was sitting down now, eager for me to enter. I prolonged his agony and hesitated. It was a little game I played with him. I waited outside the door for a few seconds, then called out to him.

"Charlie. Daddy's home."

He started to whine through the wooden barrier, unable to contain his canine emotions. I ended the torture and opened the door, bracing myself for the inevitable bum rush. I should have trained him not to jump up on me when I came home, but I never had the heart. He seemed so genuinely happy to see me that I was unable to take that behavior away from him.

As the door swung open, he sat on the other side, just like I thought. Any second now he would come bounding into the breezeway to tackle me. But he didn't.

He stayed a few feet inside the door staring at me, his ears flat against his head. Something was wrong. A ball of fear formed in the pit of my stomach. This wasn't like him.

"Come here, boy," I said and stepped forward, holding my hand out.

Instead of coming to me, Charlie stood up on all fours, hung his head low, and growled. His fur bristled from the back of his neck to the tip of his tail. He bared his teeth at me. He'd never done that before, not even when we played rough. Instinct told me to back away, but I held my ground. If I even hinted at retreat, my authority over him as master would be threatened. Try as we might to tame our pet animals, the wild beasts of their ancestors remained just beneath the surface, ready to revert to their primal nature.

"Charlie, stop it!" I shouted and pointed at him in an effort to exert my command over him.

But he didn't back down. Instead of retreating, or at least no longer appearing threatened, he stood his ground. The snarl grew deeper, he dropped his head lower, and his eyes never left mine. His sharp white teeth gleamed in the light from the entryway. I'd never been afraid of my dog before, but a small trickle of fear urged me to retreat. Ignoring the flight response, I held my own gaze with his, assuring him that I was the dominant party in this relationship. He continued to growl. A thin line of drool ran down the side of his mouth to the wood floor. It hit the surface with a wet slap.

"Charlie. No."

I took a step forward, still pointing, not really knowing if that was the right thing to do. But he was my dog and I was his master. My only thought was to do whatever I could to make him obey my commands.

Instead of backing down, he lowered his head a

little further and let out a couple of sharp barks, warning me to stay back. I stopped, preparing myself for an attack. It was strange to think that he would attack because he never exhibited the slightest hint of non-play aggression toward me. He'd bark and snarl at strangers, of course. But any dog worth its salt - even little ankle biters - are defensive of their pack. We both held our ground.

Charlie snarled and barked one more time, then whimpered and seemed to come to his senses. He trotted into the breezeway to my side. His head nudged against my hand, and he gave it a lick. I patted him on the head.

"Good boy," I said, then crouched down to meet him at eye level. "What got into you, boy?" Of course, there was no answer.

I stood and walked into the house. Charlie followed me like my own shadow, panting a little. I shut the door behind me, shrugged off my jacket, and hung it on the hook. I was surprised to see the time that flashed at me on the microwave mounted over the stove. It had been over two hours since I left work. On a normal day, it took me twenty-five to thirty minutes to drive home, less if I drove fast. I marveled at the loss of over ninety minutes. The entire episode with the spinning disc of lights could have lasted no more than ten, maybe fifteen minutes at most. Where did more than an hour go?

I continued toward the dining room, passing to the left of the table that had sat in the same spot for generations. It was solid oak, had been refinished many times over, and was overdue for another round. The chairs were original as well; the only addition was copious amounts of wood glue that was used to fix the variety of parts that had broken over the years, much of it due to me and my sister's carelessness as children.

The silver torch lamp with the white plastic shade

that glowed in the corner of the living room had not been in my family for generations. It was just a cheap piece I picked up at a yard sale for the sole purpose of lighting up the front window. It looked out of place in the midst of the collection of furnishings that were either antique or just plain old.

The ominous feeling I had earlier did not subside. I was paranoid about what might be around any corner of my old house. It was too quiet.

To break up the silence, I walked over to the coffee table that was cluttered with junk mail, grabbed the remote, and turned on the television. That was another modern convenience that clashed with the rest of the otherwise rustic décor. The bright forty six inch screen lit up. I was too far out in the sticks to get cable, but the satellite I'd installed a few years earlier worked perfectly. The news channel I left on most of the time droned on about politics, financial news, and wars so far removed from me that they did not even seem possible. I ignored it like I always did and walked out of the room, just grateful to hear the sound of anything.

Beyond the living room was a formal parlor that I never entered, except to do a twice a year cleaning. It was furnished in the same way my mother had left it, as a sitting room that never hosted any guests. There was an ornate sofa, loveseat, and chair upholstered with a delicate rose fabric. The arms and feet were carved mahogany in an elegant pattern. In the middle of the room sat an equally opulent mahogany coffee table. In front of that was a formidable brick fireplace. It was so large that it seemed incapable of producing enough heat to make it useful. The chimney had been purposely plugged up.

I passed by this room on my way to the stairs that

led to the second floor. It was an odd setup. In most contemporary homes the stairs were made into a sort of focal point of the room, something interesting to look at in otherwise dull surroundings. But this staircase was hidden in the back like some unseemly secret; as though to reveal how a person might ascend to the second level was a mystery best left undiscovered.

I flipped the light on at the bottom of the stairs and walked up. The steps were creaky but solid. The carpet runner was worn in the middle and should have been replaced or ripped out years ago. The banister and baseboard molding were made from the most solid wood of their day, unlike the cheap wood and building materials used to toss together most of the shiny new toothpick mansions that were so abundant in Avondale.

The single bathroom was at the top of the stairs, along with three bedrooms; two on the right, and one on the left. I occupied the one on the left, the one closest to the bathroom. The two on the right were empty and kept closed, cleaned on the same bi-annual schedule as the parlor. In the middle of the ceiling in the short hallway leading to the two bedrooms on the right was an attic door. I never went up there, not even to clean. There were a few chests of old clothes and other assorted junk. To me, it was as though that cramped space above my head did not even exist.

I opened the door to the bathroom, flipped on the light, and stepped in. Before sitting on the toilet, I looked at myself in the small mirror above the sink. I looked haggard. My stubble, shaved just the day before, had begun to show. I dragged my hand across my chin. It felt like sandpaper. I turned my head from one side to the other. My nose was more or less straight and proportionate for my face. Not too big, and not too small. My mud-colored eyes were bloodshot from exhaustion and stress. I took off my hat to look at my hair, which had taken to receding. The loss was nothing too noticeable, but disconcerting nonetheless.

I turned away from the mirror and sat down to use the toilet. When I was done, I washed my hands and considered taking a shower before going to sleep. The old claw foot tub was shrouded in a milky plastic curtain. I pulled back the curtain and looked at the hot and cold knobs that gleamed dully. No sir, they didn't make them like this anymore. Too tired to consider the effort of cleaning up worth the time, I closed the curtain and walked back into the hallway.

I turned left toward my bedroom door. When I opened it, the dark cave of my room never looked more inviting. The blackout curtains I'd hung doubled the darkness in the room. I hardly needed them at night, but since I slept through most of the morning I kept them shut at all times to block out the morning sun. The light from the hall barely penetrated the near pitch blackness.

I heard the sound of dog nails click-clacking against the wood floor on the first floor, followed by rhythmic padding up the stairs as Charlie rushed to join me. He weaved past me into the darkness of the bedroom. I heard him rustling around, digging at his blanket and bed. He'd slept in the same room as me since he was a puppy. At first, I made him sleep in a crate by the side of the bed. About a year later, I moved onto making him sleep in his own bed on the floor. There were many nights that he tried slipping into bed with me, but I never once relented. Each time he tried, back to the crate he'd go for the night until he learned his lesson.

I entered the room and closed the door behind me. The feeble light from the hall was no match for the

40

absence of light in my room. It didn't matter, though. I knew my way around the room in the dark, having memorized the layout after years of navigating the space blind. Before collapsing into bed, I turned on the pedestal fan in the corner of the room, both to blow air around the room and to make white noise.

I took off my shirt as I walked to the bed, and tossed it on the floor. I sat down on the mattress, unbuttoned my pants, and stripped down to my underwear. In one fluid motion, I slipped beneath the cool cotton sheets and light comforter. After laying my head on an equally cool pillow, I fell easily into sleep. The last thing I heard was a grunt from Charlie as he plopped into place on his bed, and then there was silence. Most nights it took me a few moments to nod off, but not that night. It wasn't surprising considering my utter exhaustion. It had been a long day.

● ● ●

I dreamed of blinding white light invading the cabin of my truck. I cowered on the center of the bench seat like I had in real life, but the light in the dream was different. It pulsed like a heartbeat, and I felt an outside force encouraging me to exit the truck. It made no sense to me, but dreams were sometimes that way, abstract yet somehow real. I saw the orange, pink, and green lights swirling clockwise around the metal disc with the inner circle of white lights spinning counterclockwise. The metal reflected the light dully, and I sensed it was cold to the touch. The low hum penetrated my bones. I was afraid it was melting my marrow, and somehow altering the essence of my being.

And then in a half blink of an eye, the spinning disk disappeared into nowhere. I got out of the truck and then everything went black.

● ● ●

I woke up in the dark, just like every other day. But unlike every other day, I was covered in a thin sheen of sweat. My bedroom felt too warm, stuffy. It was hard to catch my breath in the thick air. I hit the button on the watch I forgot to take off before bed, making its digital face glow. The black letters surrounded by a soothing blue light told me that I'd only been asleep a couple of hours. I knew then that it would be a long night. I lay my head back down on the pillow and moaned, having no idea how I would ever get back to sleep. My mind replayed the dream and the events that inspired it.

The glow from my watch winked out, and in the darkness, I felt that there was something in the room beyond my impaired vision; something alive that teemed with a subdued malevolence I couldn't explain. I'd never been scared of the dark. In fact, I embraced it. Unlike other children, I believed my parents when they told me the dark was just like the day, but with no light. But now I felt what all the kids who were scared of the dark had described. Something was there just beyond my reach, watching and waiting to pounce. It was a terrible, lonely feeling, being the only person awake for miles, except for maybe Bill Conder, an insomniac who owned the dairy farm north of my farmhouse.

A cool breeze not from the fan tickled my ear. That was enough for me. I switched on the bedside lamp. Its light was absorbed by the black shades and had a hard time illuminating much of the room. I looked around, searching the shadows for the source of my uneasiness. My imagination would not have needed much encouragement to make the leap to seeing a monster in every shifting shadow. But there was no monster. Everything was as it should have been, or at least where I last remembered it. I wasn't exactly a tidy person, but I knew where all of my scattered belongings had landed. None of the piles I saw around the room were unknown to me.

Despite confirming that there was nothing to be afraid of, I still wasn't comfortable. The light from the lamp burned too bright and for a moment I wish I'd never bought the blackout curtains. The contrast between light and dark was too sharp. The curtains seemed like such a good idea at the time I bought them and had served me well for years. I lay back down, turned on my side and stared at the lamp, wondering if I'd have the courage to turn it off or to ever sleep again.

Against my usual better judgement, I called out to my dog. I didn't care. I needed the comfort, even if it was just from a dog. "Charlie. Come here, boy."

I heard him rustle and growl a little in his sleep in response to my command, but he did not move. I called again, louder, more forceful. "Charlie. Come here, boy."

That got his attention. He came around the side of the bed and stared at me, puzzled. It didn't take much convincing to make him rebel against years of training. I patted the mattress beside me, and he took a great leap over my body. He plopped down on top of the blankets with his back to mine and fell asleep right away.

One thing that brought me a measure of comfort was that Charlie had not sensed anything off in the room. If he had, the racket he'd cause would scare away anything within ten miles. I still didn't feel quite right, but I managed to fall asleep staring at the burning light that fought to dispel the darkness, wishing for the sun to rise.

• 3 •

The following night I was alone for my shift at Avondale Farms. My partner had called in again, and I had the feeling he wasn't ever coming back to work. He'd either found a different job he liked better, or more likely, had decided that unemployment suited him best. What that meant for me was that it would take an eternity before a replacement was found. I used to prefer going solo, but that night I could have used the company.

I'd made a few rounds of the property during the daylight portion of my shift and was just coming back to the guard shack when the last of the employees pulled up to the gate. It was the head of the company, Mr. Pierson, burning the six o'clock oil. He was a third generation owner of Avondale Farms, as well as the associated fruit processing plant and it showed. While he was usually pleasant to those around him he possessed an air of entitlement that his daddy and granddaddy before him did not. I pressed the button to open the gate and gave him a friendly wave as he drove past me. He smiled and waved back, which seemed nice, but I had the feeling I was no more significant than an ant in his life. The gate screeched to a close after he passed through it. I watched his car turn out of the driveway and make its way down the road toward the uppity section of Avondale.

I tried not to notice the sun as it hovered dangerously close to the tree line. The sky had darkened to a deeper shade of blue above the subtle warm glow of the vanishing sun. A few purple and pink clouds floated across the sky. My mouth felt dry as I realized it would be fully dark the next time I made my rounds. The thought of walking around the building in the dark by myself left me feeling vulnerable. I'd never been nervous doing my rounds before, just like I'd never been scared of the dark. Cautious always, but never nervous. I was treading into unfamiliar emotional territory.

In order to avoid walking around in the dark, I made the next round a half an hour early, before the sun fully disappeared. And even then I made quick work of it. As I power-walked around the factory I wanted nothing more than to get back to the relative comfort of the lighted guard shack.

After the sunlight faded the stars popped out. I knew I would have to make the first of my post-sunset rounds soon. My dry mouth was accompanied by a creeping dread that radiated from my stomach into my chest and throat. I decided to skip the next perimeter check instead of facing my growing fear.

When another hour passed I knew I couldn't put off the long walk any longer. I stood up from the chair, zipped up my jacket, and grabbed the flashlight. I noticed a slight tremor in the hand holding the flashlight. Once I discovered the shaking in my hand, I realized I was trembling all over. It had nothing to do with the chill in the air, despite the fact that it was colder that night than I had expected. I'd never literally shaken with fear before. And it was most certainly fear that drove the rumbling in my body. My stomach growled and my bowels clenched. I had to get a hold of myself.

After grabbing the keys to the guard shack off the hook by the door, I decided to just rip off the Band-Aid and make my rounds. I'd never backed down from anything out of fear or anxiety and wasn't about to start. Aside from stubbornness, my upbringing would also never allow me to cower inside, pretending that I'd gone outside in the dark when I never did. I had my integrity to consider.

I had just turned the corner to walk the long backside of the factory when I heard a rustling on the other side of the tree line ahead and to my left. I froze in place and pointed the flashlight toward the source of the noise. The leaves of the bushes low to the ground moved. My throat clenched. The bushes opened, and a young deer walked out of the forest and stepped into a clearing between the fence and the woods surrounding the property. It was too young to tell if it was a buck or a doe, but it had clearly been born earlier that spring. Its telltale spots had not yet faded. I exhaled and relaxed my grip on the flashlight.

The fawn regarded me for a moment, looking at me with keen interest. It took a step toward the fence, sniffing the air ahead of it. I made no move toward the animal. I just watched it doing what it did, fascinated by its naïve nature. In a little over six months, this gentle creature would be running for its life from bloodthirsty hunters. Don't get me wrong. I support hunting and love a good venison steak or roast, as well as the next person.

But watching the deer approach the fence unafraid, I couldn't help but think about how its perspective of man would change once fear was introduced.

After a few more seconds of mutual silent appreciation, the deer dipped its head and trotted back into the woods. I continued my rounds, forcing myself to slow down. I wanted nothing more than to sprint back to my refuge of relative safety – which let's face it, was nothing more than a thin-walled, thrown together afterthought that offered little actual protection.

While walking the last stretch on the other side of the factory, I looked at the sky. The moon hovered above the tree line to the east, a little over half full. The stars twinkled in their magical way. It was no wonder to me how the ancients could have developed the mythologies they did after viewing the vast, intimidating expanse of sparkling silence night after night.

A swift movement of light caught my attention. Several glowing contrails streaked across the sky a few degrees south of the moon. It reminded me of shooting stars I had seen with my dad when I was younger, but these were different. Shooting stars were fast, burning bright and disappearing almost as soon as I spotted them. What I saw were a cluster of objects, maybe half a dozen or so, moving at a brisk pace across the sky, but not burning out. Perhaps they were remnants of some larger object that had broken apart during its entry into the atmosphere. That explanation could have worked if their luminosity lost some intensity, but they did not.

A prickle ran up the back of my leg and memories of what I had seen the night before rushed to the forefront of my mind. Instead of maintaining my slow intentional pace, I shifted to a brisk walk. It wasn't long before the prickle moved from my legs to my spine, causing a shiver. It was the same sensation as someone walking across my grave, as the old-timers would say. The corner at the end of the long side of the building loomed ahead. My brisk walk became a speed walk.

I'd made it three-quarters of the way down the far short side of the building when I spotted the guard shack in the distance. The exterior and interior lights of the small structure shone like a beacon, beckoning me to the safety of its four walls. My heart beat faster and I started a little jog. When I was about halfway between the building and the shack, I pumped my legs harder and sprinted as fast as I could. I'm not sure if it was just my imagination, but I felt a presence closing in on me from behind, perhaps hoping to take me by surprise. I refused to look back to confirm my suspicions.

I was panting by the time I reached the door to the shack. I dug the keys out of my pocket and fumbled with them, frustrated as I felt there was no time to waste. I still refused to look behind me. The feeling of being pursued grew stronger. Too strong for me to think clearly. I somehow found the right key with my shaking hand and unlocked the door. I opened and closed it within what felt like the same second. In the next second, I locked the door and the deadbolt. I backed away, averting my eyes from the glass all around me, convinced that I would see whatever I sensed had chased me from behind the factory. I reasoned that if I was unable to acknowledge its existence with my five senses, it would somehow not exist.

I dared a glance out the window in the door. The light in the shack created a slight mirroring effect, but there were enough floodlights surrounding the building to allow me a pretty good view. There was no monstrous beast hulking in the field, waiting for me to make a false

49

move, just high grass surrounding the well-worn trail that led to the north side of the building. I let out a ragged breath of relief, expelling most of my unfounded fear. I noticed I was trembling again and sat down in the chair like a dead weight.

I looked at the window in front of the desk, and due to the mirroring effect noticed my face was slick with sweat. I ran a hand across my brow. It came away wet. I hadn't even realized I was perspiring. The cold sweat reminded me of my dream the night before, which led to thinking about the spinning disc with the gyrating lights. I felt myself slip into unfamiliar feelings of paranoia and fear.

"Get a hold of yourself, Alex," I said out loud, surprised by the weakness in my own voice.

As I began to regain control of my psyche, the fluorescent light bar above my head flickered, sending a fresh wave of panic radiating from my stomach to the tips of my fingers and toes. Flickering lights were never a good sign. Every part of my body felt charged with nervous electricity. The light flickered a second time, and I was afraid it would go out and I'd be left in the dark.

But you're not afraid of the dark, I tried to tell myself.

Yes, you are, another voice, which was also mine, whispered into my ear.

I closed my eyes and braced myself for the blackout. Heaven knows they happened plenty out in the sticks. Thunderstorms, snow storms, wind storms, a downed tree, and countless unplanned events had the potential to cause a chain of events that could bring down a power line or transformer and put the greater part of Forest County out of commission. Most of us were smart enough to invest in generators and have wood-burning fireplaces with plenty of wood stocked up in case the power quit. But there was still an uncomfortable sense of being disconnected from civilization as a whole when it did happen.

Too much time had passed for it to be a full power failure. I could tell the lights had stayed on through my closed eyelids. I opened them to slits and allowed myself another great exhale of relief. I shook even harder than before from the adrenaline that rushed through my body. If there was a person trapped under a car, I'm sure I would have had the superhuman strength to lift it off of them.

As my heart and mind returned to a relative state of normal, I felt sick to my stomach. I grabbed the garbage can under the desk, prepared to throw up into it with gusto. I felt hot in the face and wished I had something cold to press to my forehead. I felt the gorge rising to the back of my throat. *Here it comes, Alex.*

But it didn't come. The nausea passed. I still felt hot and clammy, so I unzipped my jacket and shed it onto the dusty floor. I pulled at the tie that was tight as a noose around my neck and unbuttoned the top two buttons of my blue shirt. The air in the guard shack was stifling. I had the thought that I should open the door and let in some fresh air, but I didn't dare expose myself to the invisible horrors that might be lying in wait for me beyond the threshold of my imagined safety zone.

A roll of paper towel caught my attention. I ripped off four pieces and folded them together into a sort of gauze-like pad. I popped the top of my water bottle and poured the cool liquid onto my makeshift compress. I held it against my forehead and could feel the heat coming off my skin through the layers of absorbent paper. I wiped my face with the paper towel in an attempt to cool it down. My stomach flipped again and my lower intestines cramped. I started to fear that I would let loose from both ends, and there was no bathroom inside the shack.

Thankfully, the feeling passed and my face returned to a more tolerable temperature. I sat down in the chair and looked at the clock. Somehow, over an hour had vanished. I decided to skip my next perimeter check. There was no way I could force myself to do it. I looked at the chart on the clipboard and felt a twinge of guilt as I checked the task off the list, knowing that twice in one night I had recorded that I did something I didn't do.

● ● ●

The next hour passed without incident. I still felt like I was dancing on the edge of a fence, but there was no razor wire to keep me on my toes, threatening a painful and bloody experience if one foot happened to slip. I decided I could do the next perimeter check. I buttoned up my shirt and moved my tie back into place. I checked my reflection in the front window to make sure my uniform was in order and noticed my face looked pale and waxy. A light purpling under my eyes made me look haunted, hollow somehow. If I hadn't been abandoned by my partner, I probably would have gone home sick. As it was, my relief would not show up for another couple of hours. I hoped John and Alicia would be on time.

I shrugged on my jacket, zipped it up and grabbed the flashlight and keys. I opened the door to the cool night air. Sometime during the last two hours, a heavy fog had descended, adding a new element to the gloom. I half considered just closing the door and waiting inside until John or Alicia arrived. But I wasn't a coward. I'd always been too proud to run away from anything. Facing problems head-on was the only way I knew how to deal with them. I knew deep down that sometimes running away was the smarter thing to do, but I could never convince myself of that.

I closed the door behind me and locked it with the key. A slight breeze rustled through the trees and grass that surrounded the large stamp of cleared property. I looked up and imagined what the factory looked like from above. It must have been a clear landmark that stood out in the middle of the dense forest.

As I passed the corner where the short and long side of the building met, I heard the sound of something heavy being dragged across wet leaves. I wondered if perhaps a bear had woken up from his long winter's nap and was out hunting for a springtime snack. I could see the beast in my mind, lumbering through the woods, bleary-eyed and groggy, with food being the only clear thought or desire in its animal brain.

The dragging noise stopped, followed by a sound best described as the pattering of children's feet against hard ground. It was unnatural in this setting.

The fear I'd pushed down earlier returned, causing a tightening in my chest and a lump in my throat. It suddenly became hard to breathe. With a shaking hand, I probed the swirling murk beyond the fence with my flashlight, hoping I wouldn't see anything at all.

In the weak beam of light, a light gray patch of color moved fast through the fog, creating a hole in the swirling mist that collapsed in on itself as the thing passed through it. The patter of little feet mixed with the squishing of wet leaves and the occasional snap of a twig. My first thought was coyote, but they were brown, not grey. And the footsteps seemed too light to be a wolf. I supposed it could have been a wolf pup, but the truth was I had no idea what I'd just seen. It was just a flash of gray. One thing I knew for sure is that I had no desire to run into anything.

I listened as the pattering of little feet faded into nothingness before I took a step toward the general direction where I'd seen the gray flash. The thickening fog was claustrophobic, yet comforting in its oppressiveness. I was able to hide from any predator that might be out there with me; however, that same predator would be hidden from me. And I had nothing more than a flashlight and the aged chain link fence as protection.

I'd heard no snarl, no growl warning me to stay away, just the sound of dragging, followed by the sound of little feet running away. A wolf or a canine would have growled or barked to warn me. And any half-starved predator would have made at least some attempt to protect its rightful kill. Wouldn't it?

I stopped again, newly afraid of what I might see through the fog with the flashlight. I hated myself for my fear. It was an unwelcome emotion that crowded out my usual general sense of emptiness and longing for something more out of my life. I started to sweat again and felt a chill shudder through my body. If it had been any other night I would have thought that I was coming down with some nasty virus. But I knew the truth. I was in danger of being paralyzed by the encroaching fear.

Faking courage I did not feel, I forced myself to take a step forward, then another, and another. I continued on in this deliberate way until I nearly stepped into something awful. And when my flashlight beam

54

landed on an animal carcass, I thought I might actually be able to vomit. I felt my gorge rise again and turned to the side, breathing deeply. Beads of perspiration dripped off my brow onto the already soggy ground. After a few seconds of concentrated effort, the nausea passed.

The dead deer, identical to the adolescent fawn I'd seen earlier, was on the ground before me. It was a doe. A fact I confirmed by what I could see of its genitalia, which was splashed with its own wet, thick blood, as was most of the rest of it. The white tail sticking out from behind was stained a bright red. I wanted to look away but felt compelled to examine it further.

The poor beast lay mostly on its back, split open from throat to pelvis. The ribcage was broken open, revealing the heart and lungs inside. The heart was a deep crimson and the lungs looked pink, fresh. The stomach cavity was also exposed, the skin peeled back and the organs inside suspended in place somehow. The stomach, liver, pancreas, and intestines were visible but had yet to spill out.

A trail of blood led away from the deer to the edge of the fog on the factory side of the fence. It took a moment for my brain to register that fact. I followed the clearly marked blood trail to the edge of the perimeter fence. There was a hole dug into the ground under the fence that was big enough for the deer and for something else to squeeze through. Something small.

I strained to see past the fence into the woods, but the fog made it impossible. I stepped toward the metal chain link barrier and peered out as far as I could. The trail of blood and the markings where the deer had been dragged across the ground were clearly visible. The thick fog cut off any further view. I thought about investigating further. It would have been easy to slip through one of the staggered locked gates around the fence and go wandering in the woods. I was curious, but not curious enough to take a stupid risk. I decided to wait until someone else was with me. I'd leave the deer for now. I couldn't move it anyway, as the usual protocol was to call animal control to dispose of it.

I hurried through the rest of the perimeter check. Aside from the gray thing, the pattering of feet, and the dead deer, there was nothing unusual. The feeling of being followed was gone, but I was still anxious. The fog helped create a false sense of security. I was able to stay hidden in it. The odds of running into a monster or a monster finding me in the swirling white mist was greater than finding the proverbial needle in a haystack.

I followed the hazy glow of the lights that I assumed were from the guard shack, but could not see the complete structure until I was within twenty yards of it. The shack emerged from the mist like a beacon of safety. I slowed my pace and listened, realizing how quiet it was outside. Aside from the crunching of my boots against the ground, there was no other sound. No crickets, frogs, or wildlife of any kind. I tried to remember if I'd heard any noises other than the dragging and the pitter patter of little feet behind the factory and couldn't. I stopped walking and struggled to listen for even the sound of a breeze disrupting the still air. There was nothing.

The newly familiar sensation of fear prickled the back of my neck and arms. I turned around in a slow circle, straining to hear anything aside from the sound of my own heart in my ears. The beat was faint at first but grew louder until the pounding of my heart was all I could hear. I recognized this as the result of my ears searching consciously for any available sound signature. I walked toward the guard shack, determined to put a barrier between myself and the night.

My heart was still beating hard after I closed and locked the door. I took a seat at the desk and peered into the impenetrable haze beyond the thin planes of glass that separated me from the outside world. Heavy fog drifted past the windows. I could feel the air around me, thick with moisture. On a night like that, the animals and insects in the woods and swamp surrounding the factory should have been going nuts. Instead, they were silent, as though they were hiding from a predator powerful enough to find and kill them all. I pushed the thought of a creature of that magnitude out of my mind and went to work, concentrating far too much on my security checklist.

· 4 ·

Another hour passed. It was time for my last perimeter check of the night. The fog was even thicker than before. A thick roiling mass of white mist boiled past the front window. Standing in front of the glass looking out, I could not see two feet in front of me. The lights from inside and outside created an eerie luminescence, as though the fog was somehow lit from the inside instead of just merely reflecting light.

As I stared out the window I heard a slight buzzing and a crackle above my head. I looked up and watched the fluorescent light bar overhead flicker and weaken, but remain lit. It was the only light in the guard shack that seemed to be in danger of winking out. It flickered once more before returning to its former brightness. My focus shifted back to the window.

A distorted orb of white light pushed through the fog from a distance, moving forward at a lethargic pace. It was so slow I wondered if I imagined its progress due to the lack of a point of reference in the murk. I closed my eyes for a few seconds and imagined the position of the strange ball of light in relation to my surroundings. The memory of the ball of light burned on the back of my eyelids in negative. When I opened my eyes, the orb was closer.

If I wanted to get a more accurate position on whatever it was that kept moving closer, I would have to kill the lights in the guard shack. I walked over to the panel near the door that controlled the inside and outside lights. Under normal circumstances, I would have just shut them off as soon as I reached the switches, but my new companion of fear caused me to hesitate. I stood there with my hand poised to cut off the source of the light as a battle raged inside me. On one hand, I was ready and willing to plunge myself into darkness to further investigate the burning light headed my way. On the other hand, the light inside gave me an illusion of safety.

Annoyed with myself for hesitating, I switched off the light, plunging the shack into darkness. I began to hear my heartbeat again, low and soft, pitter pattering to the pace of my fear. In another act of conscious bravery, I turned toward the glowing orb that appeared to move faster toward me. I felt the shaking return in my hands first. After that, the tremors moved to the rest of my body. Perspiration formed on my face and in my armpits as I broke out in a cold sweat of fear.

The floodlights outside the gates and the glowing orb were the only things visible through the thick fog. The single disembodied light grew larger and brighter. At first, I thought it might have been a motorcycle headlight, but a person would have needed a death wish to ride a bike in near zero visibility.

I turned the inside lights back on and waited as

the light grew closer. The orb hesitated for the briefest of moments before continuing. I looked at the door, wondering if it would do any good to make a run for it before whatever was out there arrived. My apprehension about what might be hiding outside in the murk besides a disembodied light kept me glued to the shack. I imagined all sorts of horrible beasties waiting to pounce on unsuspecting prey.

I started to pace the cheap linoleum floor, weighing my options. I was not armed, having left my gun at home, but I did have experience in security. Not that I meant much. I was responsible for walking around the inside of a fenced in fruit factory and reporting anything odd to someone who could actually do something about it. I was nothing more than a messenger spy. I thought of running again. The sound of an approaching engine changed my mind.

I looked out the window and recognized Alicia's four-door beater sedan, which had a single working headlight, the source of the mysterious orb. I breathed a sigh of relief and felt ridiculous for thinking it was something else.

Her car was once a very pretty blue color but had become pockmarked with rust and numerous dents. It looked as if the whole thing was ready to fall apart, much like my truck. No one ever said the career choice of security was lucrative. The one thing the car had going for it was Alicia's mechanic husband. The engine and all the parts that made the car run were tuned to perfection.

I pressed the button for the gate, which started its long journey along the track, squeaking and squealing until it came to a stop. Alicia drove her car through the entrance and parked on the back side of the guard shack, out of sight. If anyone on the day shift at the factory ever saw her eyesore of a vehicle, they would be sure to let her know about it. God knows I took my share of verbal abuse over my choice of transportation.

The engine went quiet. I sat in one of the two chairs in the shack and waited for Alicia to knock on the door. I struggled to appear calm, but the trembling and cold sweat betrayed me. I had to hold it together long enough to get through the last hour of my shift. Why was Alicia so early? It was her habit to roll into work just on time, or late.

Despite knowing she was on the way to the guard shack, I was still startled when she knocked on the door. I saw her through the window at the top of the door. Her dull brown hair was pulled back into the same severe bun I'd seen it in for years. Aside from a few more lines on her face than when she first started working at Avondale Farms, she looked the same. Her figure was solid and ample, but not fat. She was a thick woman who knew what she was and took pleasure in throwing her weight around.

I opened the door and let her in. She closed and locked it behind her. "Spooky night, isn't it, Alex?"

"Yes. This fog is crazy. I can't believe you could drive in it."

She sat down in a chair. "I know. I thought I was going to be late again."

"Aren't you early?" I gave her a perplexed look.

She sighed. "Yes, I am. But I figure out of all the nights you've covered for me, the least I could do is be early at least one time. I don't plan on making it a habit, so don't get any big ideas, but I had the opportunity and felt like I should try to pay you back in some small way."

It was actually very thoughtful of her. There were not many times in that thankless job where anyone had extended kindness to me just for the sake of it. I was touched, but my pride prevented me from doing anything more than offering her a cursory "thank you".

Changing the subject and moving away from any awkward emotional moment, Alicia spoke. "Hey, do you think we should do the last of your rounds together?"

"Yes, let's go. In fact, I need to check on a dead deer I found inside the fence. It was there an hour ago, and it looked like something got it good."

Alicia showed no sign of fear or retreat. "Sure. Let's have a look at this deer. If it's not in too bad of shape, I might consider bringing it home to my husband. Been a long time since we had any venison, and any kind of meat besides ground turkey and hamburger is pretty rare in our house."

I didn't respond to her request to take the body of the deer and put it up in her freezer. If she still wanted it by the time we got to the poor animal, I was okay with her taking it to feed her family. It wasn't protocol, but at night no one was around to hold us accountable. Of course, agreeing with her request also meant I'd have to help her carry it back and stow it in her trunk.

We left the guard shack and walked in silence, admiring the uncomfortable blinding and quiet nature of the strange mist that swirled around us. There was a quality to the fog that seemed otherworldly. The only sounds were the crunching of our feet on the ground. I waited to see if she would notice the lack of ambient noise, but she didn't. As we got closer to where I had seen the gutted deer, I slowed down and trained my flashlight on where my memory last placed the poor animal. There was no deer.

Not only was there no deer, but there was also no trail of blood, no disturbed leaves, and no hole under the fence. I walked right up to the chain link fence and pointed my flashlight toward the woods. It barely penetrated the gloom. There was no sign that anything had been there at all. That prickly feeling of fear returned to my spine.

Alicia shifted her weight and looked at me. "Are you sure it was here, Alex? It's so hard to see, maybe it's somewhere else."

I almost forgot Alicia was with me. Possibilities of what might have happened to the deer invaded my thoughts. Her voice sucked me out of the vortex of my own head. I considered what she'd said. Maybe I was in the wrong place. I walked over to her and surveyed my surroundings before I spoke my thoughts. "This was the place. I'm positive."

She gave me a sideways glance and crossed her arms. "If that's the case where's all the blood?"

Her words cast doubt into my mind again. I shook my head and kicked at the ground, thinking that by doing so I would somehow discover another ground – the true ground – beneath the surface of the dirt. I was disappointed. There was no hidden ground. I mumbled "I don't know" to myself.

Alicia shifted, communicating a growing impatience with me. I wanted to investigate every piece of this latest puzzle, hoping to find some clue that would unravel the mystery. I knew what I saw earlier. I also knew what I heard. Even if I had imagined the dead deer, could I have also imagined the dragging noises and the scurrying of little feet? I supposed it was possible, but I'd never experienced anything like that before. I could usually rely on my senses.

We walked the rest of the way back to the shack in silence, staying close to the fence. I swept the ground with my flashlight, knowing that we had long passed the location where I'd found the deer earlier. I began to doubt the validity of my memory, which had never failed me before, especially not with such a visceral experience. I knew some people claimed to have dreams so real they could feel the breeze on their skin, smell the decaying leaves in the air, and feel pain. But not me. Much like the rest of my life, my dreams were rare, and almost always in black and white. The dream from the night before was an anomaly, a fact that was not lost on me.

When we got back to the guard shack, Alicia and I sat in the desk chairs in silence. I could tell she wanted to say something to accompany the look of pity on her face. I had little interest in having her condescend to me with a pat on the back and a *There, there. Everything will be okay, Alex. Maybe you just need to lie down.*

I spoke first. "I'm not crazy. I know what I saw. There was a deer gutted – practically filleted – out there behind the factory. I heard something drag it across the ground and then the sound of something else running away."

Alicia became defensive. "I never said you were crazy. If you say you saw something out there, I believe you. It's just that without seeing it myself, it's hard for me to fully accept what you're saying. I'm sure you can understand that."

We stared at each other for a long moment. I held my gaze, daring her to look away. But she didn't. She held fast to her side of the staring contest.

I'm sure I told you that she is pretty stubborn. And if I hadn't before, I'm telling you now. Alicia was the most bull-headed person I'd ever met in my life. If she got it into her mind to anchor herself to a position on any topic it was nearly impossible to move her away from it.

I broke my gaze first and slumped my shoulders forward, admitting defeat. "I know what you're saying. I have to admit that I would think the same thing if you had told me. I'd think you had lost a few marbles or popped a few screws loose. I don't blame you for thinking it about me."

Her face softened and she gave a little nervous laugh. "Alex, I never meant to insult you. I just wanted to be honest. And quite frankly this fog is creeping me out. I'm almost glad there was nothing out there for us to see."

I nodded and turned away to stare out the window. I can't remember why I was seized by the sudden urge to tell her about what I saw the night before. It was a strong pull, this need to share my experience with another person. I was scared of rejection and more pity, but I also knew that Alicia was open to the supernatural. She'd told me her fair share of ghost stories over the years. The more I tried to push the feeling away, the more it persisted.

I turned around in the chair to face her. My heart pounded and I felt the birth pains of a stress headache coming on. I had a tale to tell, along with a captive and semi-willing audience. I exhaled sharply through my nose and leaned back in the chair. Alicia tilted her head to the side with a question in her eyes, perhaps a rhetorical *Are you alright?* already forming in her mind.

I preempted the inquiry. "I saw something last night on my way home. Something I can't explain." I paused. "I don't really want to tell you this, but I think you are just about the only person who might listen to me without making me feel completely insane."

My words piqued her interest and her eyes lit up with the expectation of wonder at an interesting tale.

"What happened?" She asked, almost breathless.

I looked at her, wondering again if I could trust her. This would be a good test. "Well, I was about halfway home and my truck started acting funny. All the lights went out and it stalled, like all the power just left it. I had to coast over to the shoulder in the dark. I sat there looking out the window into the near pitch black, wondering what happened. I was a good ten miles from home and had no interest in walking that far. I had just reached back behind the seat to pull out my emergency kit when the radio, and just the radio, blared to life with the sound of static."

Alicia looked incredulous. She cocked her head and lifted her brow. "Alex, come on. That radio hasn't worked for as long as I've known you. Now stop pulling my leg, or I…"

I interrupted her. "I'm telling you the God's honest truth. The radio just came on. It didn't matter which station I chose, there was nothing but this weird, pulsing static. And then the whole cabin of the truck filled with a bright white light. I'm not sure if it was because of the adjustment from darkness to light, but it seemed like the strength of a thousand of those sickening LED lights. It was hard to find the trace of a shadow for comfort."

I had her attention. She leaned forward in the chair, the glimmer in her eyes encouraging me to go on.

"A low humming sound kicked up soon after. The vibration was so low that I could feel it all the way to my bones. And then the bright white light blinked out and I could see softer pulsating lights. White, orange and pink moved across the dashboard and hood of my truck. I got out to take a look. About a hundred feet up, there were two sets of lights spinning against each other like the gears of a clock."

I left out all the cowardly parts. Perhaps some will judge me for my vanity, but it was my tale to tell after all, wasn't it? In any case, she was enraptured by my story. I saw the excitement behind her eyes, the hunger to know more, to know what happened next.

"I stared at the thing hanging in the sky for a little bit and then it just disappeared in a flash. If I had blinked I would have missed it streaking across the sky from one horizon to the other. I've been trying to convince myself that I didn't see what I saw, that it was somehow my imagination, but I think I saw an honest to goodness UFO."

Alicia's mouth gaped open. Her eyes were wide and filled with mischief. "Are you for real, Alex? Are you telling me you had a close encounter of the first kind?"

"If you're asking if I think I saw a UFO, then yes." It felt strange to speak it out loud. I had been trying to suppress the truth in my mind, hoping that I just imagined the whole thing. But my experience was undeniable.

Something about what Alicia asked struck me. "Are there any other kinds of close encounters?"

Alicia gave me an *Are you serious?* look, and I was close to wanting to slap it off her face. I twisted in my seat while she responded, counting off the types of encounters on her fingers. "There are at least five that I am aware of. Let's see, there's the first kind, which is a sighting, second is physical evidence, third is an alien encounter, fourth is abduction, and the fifth is two-way communication. Did you see anything else last night?"

"No, thank God. I have no interest in experiencing encounters of any kind." How stupid and naïve I was at that time.

Alicia's face twisted into a grimace. It looked like she might have a conniption fit. "I wish I could have them all. That would be so epic."

I rolled my eyes and laughed at her excitement in a mocking tone, which offended her. In any case, the message I sent was clear. I had no interest in any further alien encounters or entertaining any thoughts of encouraging such an experience. A sighting of some strange flying saucer above my head was enough otherworldly excitement for a lifetime. E.T. could stay right where he was. No need to phone home if you never leave the mother ship. And I'll keep my Reese's Pieces to myself.

I sat with Alicia in silence until her partner John arrived on time by some miracle. It was the first time in weeks that I was able to leave by the end of my scheduled shift. I said my goodbyes in a hurry. John was friendly and returned in kind, but Alicia ignored me. I wanted to tell her I was sorry for insulting her, but the truth was I wasn't. My entire being revolted against the idea of continuing to experience something outside the realm of what I considered to be normal. I would not have her encouraging me to dive deeper into the mysteries of the unknown. As the two of them set off for their first perimeter check of the night, I drove off in my truck.

• 5 •

Gravel spit out from the back of the tires as I pulled away from the factory. I was angry with myself for telling Alicia about my encounter, but I was even more upset about alienating someone who could have been a confidant by being a jerk. But the truth was that I didn't want anything else to do with UFOs. I wanted to push what had happened deep down inside and bury it inside a coffin encased in a sarcophagus beneath twenty feet of dirt. That was how desperate I was to suppress the truth. But truth has a way of resurrecting itself from the most brilliantly constructed cages.

I drove home slower than normal. Too slow to justify gripping the steering wheel so tight that my knuckles were white. It would take an hour to get home at that pace, and the thick fog was no excuse. Frustrated, I punched the gas and tried to force my way through my anxiety. The memory of the night before burned into my subconscious and I was helpless to fight its effects on my waking thoughts. My palms started to sweat.

I made it about five miles when I had to pull over to the side of the road. I shifted the truck into neutral, put on the parking brake, and rolled down the window to let in some fresh air. I put my head against the steering wheel and struggled to calm the flurry of unwanted thoughts invading my brain.

Breathe in.

Breathe out.

Breathe in.

Breathe out.

Calm enough to try driving again, I popped the parking brake and shifted into first gear. At ten miles an hour, I shifted into second, and at twenty to third. I made it all the way to fourth gear and fifty miles an hour before I let off the gas and shifted back into third. Thirty-five was better than what I had been doing before I stopped, but I knew I was giving into the fear. And I hated myself for it.

As I drove closer to the scene of my close encounter of the first kind, I experienced a surge of anxiety and fought the urge to pull over to the side of the road again. I struggled in vain against the enormous internal pressure as I cruised onto the shoulder. My chest was tight and my world started to waver as tears clouded my vision. I pressed hard on the brake and gripped the steering wheel, willing myself to take my thoughts captive, to shove them back into their box. I put the truck in neutral and pressed down the parking brake in case I passed out from hyperventilation. I had no desire to drift into a ditch and have to walk miles home in the dark.

After allowing myself some time to breathe, my heartbeat slowed and my world stopped its mad spiral into insanity. I looked out the windshield at the visible swath of road ahead and the little bit of forest illuminated by the headlights. There was nothing but blacktop that had turned a light grey due to weather and salt over several seasons, the dirt on the side of the road, and the new green of plants coming back to life. I did not register this right away, but the fog was less dense in this section of woods.

I released the parking brake, pushed the clutch to the floor, and shifted into first gear. I slowly worked my way back up to fourth. Thirty-five to forty miles an hour wasn't anywhere near the speed limit of fifty-five, but it was better than twenty. At that pace, I'd make it home in just under fifteen minutes. I held the steering wheel a little more loosely and allowed myself to sit back against the seat. That lasted all of five minutes.

I scanned the road ahead. It was not unusual for me to make the trip home without seeing another car or creature. I called that time of day the in-between. Once in a while, I'd see a deer, rabbit, or some other animal suffering from insomnia that wandered too close to the road. The headlights and the sound of my truck were enough to scare them away most of the time.

As I continued driving near forty miles an hour, I saw what looked like the shine of animal eyes reflected in the headlights through the swirling fog. The sight of that natural phenomenon was an eerie reality. Critters got too close the road sometimes, looking for food or a good place to cross. The difference between those eyes and the ones I saw that night was stark. The orbs reflected in the headlights that night were the size of small saucers.

I let my foot off the gas and shifted into third gear. The eyes in the distance remained pointed in my direction, unblinking. I wondered if they were even really eyes at all. Some of the safety reflectors installed on high poles resembled that animal eye shine. They were usually

73

placed higher up, for the county plows to be able to tell where the road ended and the forest began in the middle of winter. The reflections I saw were well below four feet.

As I came closer to the shining eyes, I slowed down to twenty-five miles an hour. The eyes grew larger by the second as I closed the distance between us. The anxiety I had rid myself of a few minutes earlier trickled back in. I shifted into second and maintained my speed at twenty miles per hour. I wanted to look away, but I was unable to tear my gaze away from those penetrating, glassy orbs floating in the darkness ahead.

When I was within a hundred yards of the source of the shine, the hint of a shape came into focus as a dark shadow set against the fog. Whatever it was stood less than four feet tall, and the size of its eyes were disproportionate to its height. Slowing down even further, I realized the eyes were large oval shapes, not circular orbs as they had seemed from far away. My grip on the steering wheel tightened.

At fifty yards, I saw more of the shape outlined by the headlights. The head was large and round, possibly hairless. The size of the head was proportionate to the eyes; too big for the body. I could not yet make out the rest of the shape to tell if it was standing on two or four legs. Four would make sense, considering the size of the head, but it would make that thing enormous. I felt by intuition that it was two-legged, defying logic.

At twenty-five yards, I confirmed the shape stood on two legs. Something that looked like thin arms hung at its sides, with too long fingers on slender, delicate looking hands. I had no idea what kind of thing out in these woods stood on two legs like that. Sometimes a bear would rear up, but bears were rare in that part of the country, and even so, no bear stayed up on two legs like that for long. And a full-grown bear was taller than four feet. One thing was certain. It was not human.

I maintained my speed at twenty miles an hour. The creature's short legs came into view. I barely noticed any of its other features as I was drawn to those eyes; eyes that burned into my soul, searching for iniquity and finding an abundance of it. I'd never felt more exposed in my life than in that moment, discovering something about myself that I'd never known before. My lack of purity and goodness was obvious. Those terrible eyes communicated that message with startling clarity.

I continued to stare at those dark pools as I closed the gap between us. The thing (I refused to call it what it was at that point) was a medium grey color. The eyes were a deep black, as though they were all pupil. If I stared too long, I felt that I could lose myself in their inky darkness. The hanging arms and spindly legs were terribly thin, almost sick looking. And I could not spot a hair of any kind on the smooth surface of its skin, confirming my earlier suspicion. As far as I could tell, it wore no clothes of any kind. And I assumed it was female, but could not see any evidence of genitalia that would reveal its sex.

As I cruised past, those penetrating dark eyes held my own, following my progress. A tingle of revulsion crawled into my stomach and I felt my intestinal track rumble. I felt accused by those eyes, unworthy of the life I lived. The faint smell of sulfur wafted in through the open windows, filling my nostrils. I guessed that it was the essence of my own soul being torched by the creature's accusing gaze.

I coasted past this curiosity and with some reluctance turned my eyes to the road ahead. A strange compulsion came over me. It was as if I was under the power of some hypnosis, doing something I wasn't completely in control of. I stopped the truck in the middle of the road and stared into the rearview mirror. The red lights illuminated the faded blacktop behind me. My instincts told me to flee, but I stayed right where I was.

I looked up into the rearview mirror and saw the shape of that thing standing by the side of the road behind me. I felt its eyes boring into mine through the reflection, holding me with a strange hypnotic power. As if sensing my unspoken desire to see it fully, the strange being stepped out onto the road. I continued to stare into the rearview mirror, unwilling to turn around and face the creature head-on. Those eerie dark eyes continued to stare back at me. It's too large head connected to the thin frail body conjured up visions of life forms from other worlds, but I refused to allow myself to consider the possibility of what I was seeing.

The mystical hold it had over me broke when it took a step toward the truck. My flight instincts punched through whatever power that thing exerted over me. I let out the clutch and punched the gas. The truck lurched forward and stalled.

I looked away from the mirror, confused. I saw the source of the problem right away. I'd forgotten that I had come to a stop in third gear. I looked back up and the thing in the mirror was closer, strolling toward me at a slow pace, unconcerned with my failure to escape. The smooth grey of its skin gleamed dully in the red brake lights. The thin line of its mouth betrayed no emotion.

Shaking, I stepped down on the clutch and turned the key forward. For a moment, I thought I may have flooded the engine because nothing happened. The only remedy, if that was the case, was to wait twenty minutes, then try to start the truck again. I did not have the luxury of time. Thankfully, the truck started right up after turning over a couple of times. The engine roared to life.

I had just started letting the clutch out again when I remembered that I was still in third gear. And though I tried, my muddled mind could not remember where to find first gear. I'd learned to drive in this truck and finding the gears should have been automatic. It was what I considered a hard stick, not at all like the new cars with their easy shifting. The ancient truck needed a forceful hand to shove it into gear. I looked in the mirror and the creature was closer, within a few yards of the tailgate. In a fluid, dream-like motion, it raised its right arm, extending those creepy long fingers toward me. My throat tightened.

I forced myself to look away and concentrate on the shifter. The diagram that showed where each gear could be found had faded away long ago. It was nothing but a smooth, dark grey surface. I was suddenly lost without a map and no idea which direction to take. Why was it so hard to remember the simplest things under stress? I cried out in frustration as the memory of how to shift hovered just beyond the reach of my consciousness.

And then something clicked. First was the gear to the uppermost left. Reverse was below that. Second was down and to the right of first, third above that, and so on. My sweating hand nearly lost its grip as I slammed the shifter into first. I pushed down on the gas and let up on the clutch in tandem. The truck took hold of the gear and rushed forward. I dared a look into the rearview mirror and wished I hadn't. The diminutive shape stood in the road with its hand still raised toward me. Nothing had changed in the expression on its face, but I felt malevolence emanating from it. I shifted into second and kept going.

The paralyzing anxiety that gripped me earlier

gave way to a new kind of panic. My survival instincts overrode everything else. I drove home at reckless speeds so fast that I am ashamed to tell how far above the speed limit I flew. The fog thickened considerably after speeding away from that section of woods, and I could have crashed the truck with one false move. All that mattered was to get as far away from that thing as I could. I still denied what I knew deep down the little monster to be.

As I turned into my driveway too fast, I slid across the gravel turning nearly sideways and spraying rocks into the lawn behind me, while the front wheels tore up the front yard ahead of me. To compensate, I cranked the wheel the other way and punched the gas. The trick worked and I was pointed in the right direction, toward the garage. My momentum carried me the rest of the way up the driveway. I slammed on the brakes to avoid crashing through the garage door.

When I came to a stop I saw a cloud of dust billow out behind me. I could hear Charlie inside the house, barking like crazy. The truck was still rocking from the sudden stop when I shifted into first gear and shut off the engine. My heart was trip hammering. Adrenaline pumped through my veins. But it was fear that coursed through my veins thicker than anything else. My eyes watered as I rested my head against the steering wheel and closed them.

Tears sprang forth, unwanted. Emotional expression was not an easy thing for me. And those tears were not the product of some squishy feeling. They were tears driven by the sheer terror of realizing that the monster under your bed is real. It's real and it has teeth sharp enough to tear your body and spirit to ribbons. My mind tore in two as I struggled to maintain my grip on the illusion of sanity and reality.

I sat like that for a while. So long that Charlie had stopped barking. So long that the motion light on the garage blinked out. As I continued to come down from my fear-fueled adrenaline high, my body felt tired, used up. I forced myself to relax and breathed in and out slowly, crowding out the world around me.

When a measure of peace replaced my fear, I pulled the keys out of the ignition and opened the door. The cabin light came on and the movement from the door activated the motion sensor floodlight on the garage. I stepped out of the truck and squinted at the brightness assaulting me. The door shut with a solid thunk.

Instead of going through the side entrance from the garage, I walked toward the front door. The light on the porch was a beacon, promising me a safe haven. The curtains on the picture window parted and I saw Charlie's excited face. His mouth was open and he panted happily. I could picture his butt swishing his tail back and forth. His master had come home and he was ready to greet me.

The creak of the first step leading to the porch startled me as I realized it was the only noise I'd heard aside from closing the truck door a moment ago. Once again, there were no crickets, no frogs, and no breeze rustling through the trees. It reminded me of the night I had my close encounter of the first kind and finding the dead deer during my security rounds at work.

A subtle dread bubbled up from the bottom of my spine. I tried to rationalize the lack of these ambient noises to the in-between hour but failed to convince myself. I hurried up the last few steps to the front door. My hands were sure and steady as I unlocked the door, opened it, stepped inside, then closed and locked it behind me in record time.

Charlie bounded up to me. Instead of chastising him I knelt down and gave him a big hug as he approached. He responded by licking my ear and most of the right side of my face. I grimaced at the wet slobber, but welcomed the show of affection from my devoted friend.

After a few moments, my dog got a hold of his puppy emotions and padded away from me, probably toward the kitchen to look for some grub. I followed him, allowing myself to forget a little bit of what I had seen earlier and what I had not been able to hear out in the yard. Still, pesky thoughts nipped at the base of my brain.

In the kitchen, Charlie sat on his haunches looking up at me with his hungry, loving eyes. I opened the cupboard to pull out his kibble and thought, not for the first time, about how obedient he was when it came to food. He could very well nose open the cupboard and help himself, but he wouldn't dream of disobeying me in that way.

I filled his food bowl and while he was crunching on the bits I refilled his water dish. Once that was done, I walked out of the kitchen, through the dining room, and into the living room. The lack of noise, aside from Charlie's noisy eating, was disconcerting. I picked the remote control up off of the coffee table and turned on the television. The news channel I'd left on the night before blared to life.

I set the remote down and walked toward the staircase that led to the second floor, flipping light switches on as I went. I climbed the creaky steps not conscious of my purpose. My mission did not become clear until I'd made it to the landing at the top of the steps and turned toward my bedroom. I had just reached the door when Charlie came up behind me. I stopped and he crossed my path, tilting his head, a question in his eyes.

I opened the door and stared into near total darkness; a darkness I had created out of my preference to blot out the light of day. I stepped inside where the light from the hall was faint and weak. A suffocating sense of oppression rushed in at me from all sides as I stood in my cave-like room. The air was thick with a certain quality that could not be described, but it was most similar to the sensation of being choked slowly.

Using the wall switch just inside the door I turned on the floor lamp. The dark curtains covering the window absorbed much of the light, bathing the room in a dull grey. The small light fought in vain to clear away the gloom. When I'd first had the idea to black out the room, I thought it was so clever to trick myself into believing it was dark when daylight burned brightly just beyond the thick veil. I could hide from the light in this room, but all I had to do was push aside one of the panels to reveal the light my own created darkness hid from me.

In semi-conscious auto-pilot, I walked over to the nearest window and moved the curtain along its track. The motion sensor flood light on the garage still burned bright, and some of that light filtered into the room. I repeated the process with the remaining three windows until the low ambient light from outside cut through the blinders of my own design. I no longer desired total darkness where shadows hid without the ability to be detected.

I walked out of the bedroom and into the bathroom. Charlie followed me to the door and stood outside, sniffing under it while I sat down on the toilet. After a few seconds, I heard him walk away, his nails click-clacking against the wood floor. I drew a warm bath, hoping to relieve the tension of the last two days. I wanted nothing more than to sleep away the things I had seen.

Naked, I slipped into the warm water. My cares seemed to leach out of me, as I put my head under the water and the muscles in my face relaxed. When I came back up I let out a big sigh and sat back against the hard porcelain. With my eyes closed, my breathing slowed and I imagined myself falling asleep. To prevent dying in some stupid way, I wrapped my big toe around the chain connected to the drain plug and pulled it up.

I sat in the tub listening to the sucking of water flowing down the drain until it was almost empty. Only then did I open my eyes and carefully stood up. I dried myself, then wrapped the towel around my waist and walked out of the bathroom. I felt like I was sleepwalking as I floated into my bedroom. My head felt heavy, clouded by exhaustion. Without getting dressed for bed, I fell onto the mattress and went to sleep almost immediately. The last thing I heard was the sound of Charlie's nails against the floor as he made his way into the room.

Two days in a row I'd seen things that had no rational explanation. At that point, I was not ready to admit the truth of what I experienced. I'd get there. Trust me. To tell the story in proper order I have to immerse myself in the experience as it happened. One thing I could not deny was that it only took those two days to become familiar with stifling fear, and a new found wariness of the dark.

• • •

In the week that followed, I removed the black curtains from my bedroom windows and replaced them with white blinds. Because of this change, I found myself waking up far too early and bought a sleep mask as a compromise. It was difficult to reverse years of subjecting myself to near pitch darkness during sleep. But I could not allow myself to be enveloped in it any longer. I figured it was better to learn to adjust to the light than to never sleep again.

Driving home from work during that week was tense, but fast. And each day was a little bit easier. It was hard to erase the memories of what I had seen from my mind, but they became less sharp. With an iron grip and bloodless knuckles, I sped as fast as I could through the forest at night, afraid of running into something more than the deer, bear, and little critters I was used to. I also avoided driving at night on my days off.

One night at the factory, Alicia came in early bearing all sorts of literature about UFOs and alien encounters. I made the mistake of telling her about the creature I saw, and she almost exploded with excitement to tell me all about what I had seen and how she was going to help me figure out what it all meant. After all, not too many people had seen both a flying saucer and an alien so close together.

Significant was the word she used to describe my experience. It didn't feel significant. It felt like a violation of something sacred.

I took the brochures and booklets she gave me and put them in the empty plastic bag that served as my lunchbox. I promised her I'd read it all later, which I did not. As soon as I got home I dumped it all into what my mother called a "forgetting drawer".

Nearly everyone has the same sort of thing. Some people call it a junk drawer. But my dear old mom thought of nothing as junk. Everything had value if you just looked hard enough. So the junk drawer became a forgetting drawer. I found half a dozen of these forgetting drawers when she passed away. And despite her insistence that nothing was junk, that was all she put in them.

• • •

It was a Wednesday just after lunch when I got around to looking at all the literature Alicia gave me. Call it curiosity, call me a glutton for punishment. I don't really care. I had the sudden desire to read all the booklets, pamphlets and fliers; to just take a look and see what they were all about. There was no doubt I would read some wacky stuff, but maybe it would bring me one step closer to understanding what had happened to me.

I pulled the forgetting drawer out and spread the paperwork across my kitchen table. My plate with half a ham and cheese sandwich, a few potato chips and a pickle sat to the side where I'd left it. I separated the papers into like-sized piles. Nearly all of the front cover artwork featured that familiar alien face with the huge round head and enormous oval eyes in a variety of neon colors. Just looking at them made me shudder. What I'd seen out in the forest was similar to these highly stylized illustrations, but much more organic and terrifying.

I sorted through the piles and made three new stacks, one for yes, one for no, and one for maybe. One of the first I picked up was a booklet called *Aliens Among Us*. I opened it and the author presented an insane theory about a big conspiracy within the Catholic Church to hide an alien messiah that was expected to descend to earth and save us all from the horrors of war, famine, and everyday life. I tossed that into the no pile.

Another one titled *Alien Autopsy* claimed to have indisputable proof that an alien had been cut up and studied at the site of the infamous alien encounter in Roswell, New Mexico. I'd read a story about that eyewitness account a while back that proved using actual medical science that the photographs were of a deformed human fetus and nothing more. Inside that pamphlet, there were also pictures of elongated skulls that were misrepresented as alien remains. The misshapen human heads only proved that people used to do stupid things to force their heads into odd shapes, a practice similar to foot binding or neck stretching.

Most of the material was either outright marketing or included advertisements to sell even more useless crap to the gullible. I was the kind of guy who became a stone when presented with an obvious sales pitch. If there was no substance to the goods being hocked, I'd politely say no until the rehearsed speech stopped and the person went away. There was one instance when a frustrated young man turned around and stormed away, calling me all sorts of unfriendly names.

As I looked at the table I realized that I wasn't going to find any answers in all that propaganda. Just as I was ready to bundle it all up and toss everything in the garbage, where true trash goes, a black and white flyer caught my eye. There was nothing flashy about it at all aside from the poorly drawn flying saucer-shaped object in the upper left-hand corner. Its simplicity was what captured my attention. *Looking for answers?* it asked. *Have you had a supernatural experience and need a safe place to talk?*

Those two sentences called to me. The questions were so simple. I held the paper in my hand and stared at the page. There was nothing explicit for sale on the ad for the Avondale Paranormal Society; just the flying saucer image, those two sentences, an address, a phone number, a blurry map, and meeting times of Wednesdays and Saturdays at 7 p.m.

I set the paper down, stood up from the table, and grabbed the trash can out of the kitchen. I swept everything Alicia had given me into it, except for that sheet of paper. The booklets, pamphlets, and assorted loose papers landed with a satisfying whoosh on top of the other garbage. I glanced back at the table to make sure the flyer was still there, then grabbed the garbage can and my lunch plate and headed back into the kitchen. I rushed past the dining room into the living room to watch some television in an attempt to distract myself. Part of me felt drawn to the paper by some unseen attractive force, and another part of me wanted to forget all about the Avondale Paranormal Society and finding out what had happened to me.

● ● ●

Another week passed and I managed to avoid that flyer. It still sat on my dining room table, but I did my best to pretend it wasn't there. I even pushed it to the side, hoping to bury it in the ever-growing pile of junk mail I refused to throw out. I felt stupid, holding onto the flyer like some sort of security blanket, a cosmic insurance policy. I should have just thrown it away, but couldn't bring myself to do it. Another mental obstacle was my inability to picture myself attending one of those meetings. I had no interest in meeting people who had similar or worse experiences than me, and God only knew what else they might share. I just wanted to forget about my encounters and move on.

● ● ●

Despite my misgivings, I felt an internal nudge to go to a meeting. It was another Wednesday, my regular day off, and I had plenty of time to make it by the 7 p.m. start time. I resisted, thinking that my day off was my time, and I wasn't about to waste it on some crackpot deviants. Still, I knew deep down that it wouldn't be a waste of time. My intuition told me there were answers to be found there. I was still desperate to deny what had happened to me, to shove the experience deep down into the darkest corners of my mind where nobody could see and nobody knew but me.

I spent most of that afternoon puttering around the house, trying again to distract myself from that little piece of paper and the upcoming meeting. What started as a niggling thought became an obsession as time ticked forward. By four 'o clock the meeting was all I could think about. I told myself I had to go, at least once, to see what the Avondale Paranormal Society was all about, and to rule it out as an option.

I took a quick shower and dressed in blue jeans and a black t-shirt. I put on my trusty running shoes and grabbed my gray hoodie off the hook by the door. Charlie looked at me with a question in his eyes. I was doing something outside of my normal routine. I patted his head as I grabbed the truck keys off the kitchen counter. I stopped at the dining room table. The stacks of papers strewn about were chaotic by anybody's standards, but I had no problem plucking out the one flyer that had been plaguing me. I folded it up and stuffed it into the pocket of my hoodie.

I walked back to the kitchen and made sure Charlie had plenty of water and an early dinner of soft food, as well as a full dish of dry food. He was wagging his tail and devouring his favorite chunks of beef slathered in gravy as I walked out the side door.

I was already driving toward Avondale when I pulled my cell phone out of my right front pocket and spoke the address of the Avondale Paranormal Society. A soothing female voice instructed me to stay the course and if I just followed her directions she would lead me on the straight and narrow path to my destination. As with most technology she expressed confidence in her programming, even when she was wrong.

An hour later, I drove into downtown Avondale. Calling the four-block stretch of shops surrounded by early nineteenth century homes a downtown was more than generous. While most of the city had surrendered to typical suburban sprawl, the good citizens of this part of town fought and clawed to retain some of its early charm.

With over an hour to go before that night's meeting of the Avondale Paranormal Society, I decided to grab a bite to eat at The Avondale, a little café hidden between the Subway and Starbucks that tried and failed to blend in with its surroundings. I ordered a burger, fries and an orange soda at the counter and sat at a two-person table in the back of the restaurant. As the fizzy citrus drink slid down my throat, my thoughts wandered to the impending meeting. I chewed the back of my lip, a nervous habit that caused a fair amount of scarring on the inside of my mouth.

After a few minutes, my number was called out and I walked back to the counter for my meal. The scent of greasy goodness drifted into my nostrils and I was sure I'd die of a heart attack from the smell alone. The burger was cooked to medium-well perfection, and the seasoned fries were better than any I'd tasted anywhere else.

My momentary distraction of the heavy meal passed. As I sat in the small café I considered calling the phone number on the flyer like I had countless times over the past week, but I didn't. It would be better to just show up to the meeting, knocking the hosts off their game a little bit with an unexpected guest. My assumption was that whoever ran those meetings would be so busy with accommodating me that I could scope out the place with a more critical eye.

A clock on the wall reminded me that there were only fifteen minutes before the meeting started. I drank the last of my orange soda and left the restaurant. The cashier and cook, who were the same frizzy-haired, rail-thin woman, nodded to me as I left. I gave her a quick wave before I ducked out the door and jogged to my truck.

I was torn. Part of me really wanted to go see what this Avondale Paranormal Society was all about, and another part of me just wanted to go home and forget about everything I'd seen. To convince myself to stay I rationalized that I had already driven the hour from home, so I might as well make an appearance and see what the meeting was all about.

Ten minutes later I was parked in front of 1275

Ashwood Lane. It was a three-story almost white Victorian house in need of some paint. It wasn't quite an eyesore, but it was apparent that maintenance was something the owners neglected on a regular basis. I drove past and parked a little farther down the street to keep my truck out of view. I stuffed my hands in my pockets as I walked slowly up the sidewalk toward the house.

My stomach clenched at the idea of the unknown inside. As I climbed the porch steps I wondered if I had the right place. There might have been two Ashwood Lanes for example, that little miss navigator got mixed up. Or maybe I misspoke when I gave my phone the address, and I was ready to go knocking on the door of an old woman who was sure to be suspicious of some unknown man walking up her steps. Neither of those things were true.

A flyer that was an exact copy of the one I left in the truck was tacked to the side of the door. I squinted my eyes to scrutinize the piece of paper, stalling for time. I had just worked up the courage to knock on the door when I heard footsteps behind me. I turned around and saw a woman with a shock of unruly white hair and wild eyes working her way across the front porch toward me. She was older, but not the suspicious old woman I imagined.

"Are you here for the meeting, Sunny Jim?" She asked in an upbeat tone tinged with a hint of something off-kilter.

There was something strange in her voice that I couldn't quite place; a kind of otherworldly quality I associated with the slightly deranged.

I realized I was staring at her for too long. "Oh, yes. I'm here for the meeting. My name is Alex Mayfield.

And you are?"

She pointed to herself and looked to either side, as though she thought I was talking to someone else. "My name's Carla. Have you been to a meeting before? You look familiar."

Now it was me who gave her the *who me?* look. "No, I've never been to a meeting before."

Her eyes brightened and she smiled wide. "Oh, we just love virgins."

Her comment took me off guard. "Excuse me."

She gave me a sly look, as though we shared the same inside joke. "First timers. New recruits. However you want to say it. Newbies."

My cheeks flushed and I knew my face turned red with embarrassment at my misinterpretation. I tried to hide the growing color by turning away, but it was no use. Carla sensed my discomfort, said nothing further about it, and turned away to open the door. So much for my plan of taking her by surprise.

"Follow me. We meet in the living room."

I wasn't sure what I expected when I walked in based on Carla's odd behavior. It seemed like a perfectly normal house. There was a small foyer with hooks for coats and a wooden bench underneath. To the right was a front parlor with a stone fireplace and comfortable looking mismatched furniture. To the left was a dining area with an ancient table that opened up to a decent sized kitchen. The smell of baking bread and cookies was intoxicating. It felt more like my grandmother's house than a place to explore the world of UFO's and aliens.

As though she had forgotten about our awkward exchange outside, Carla motioned toward the parlor. "Have a seat anywhere you like. Would you like any coffee or anything?"

"Yes, please. Coffee with two creams and two sugars. Thank you."

"You're welcome", she said and shuffled past me toward the kitchen. I took a seat on a plaid patterned overstuffed armchair situated at the corner of the fireplace. Two sofas sat on either side of a massive dark stained oak coffee table. One was a deep chocolate microfiber, and the other upholstered in a 70's light green. Based on the seating arrangements, I estimated there would be room for no more than seven people, an intimate group.

While I waited for Carla to return with the coffee, I looked around at the kitschy décor spread everywhere. Things were arranged in a way that appeared haphazard at first glance, but there was an obvious pattern that was hard for me to grasp. There were handcrafted knickknacks intermingled with brushed steel light fixtures and lacy curtains. The style was a mix of old and new, with some of the mashups fitting well, while others would send an interior designer over the edge. It was clear that Carla was split between hanging onto the old and embracing the new.

I was just on the cusp of beginning an analysis of my host based on her decorating choices when Carla returned with the steaming cup of coffee. I gladly accepted it and leaned forward in the chair. She smiled at me and took a seat on the dark brown sofa. I took a tentative sip of the coffee. It was piping hot, delicious, with a bold, nutty flavor and a slight burnt taste. I took a bigger drink and set the cup down on the dark oak coffee table. It was better than some of the best-known coffees around. "This coffee is wonderful, Carla. Thank you."

"Oh, it's nothing sugar," she said and waved her hand in the air, seeming distracted by her own thoughts.

Carla glanced at her watch. "It looks like it might just be us, Alex. I was expecting at least a couple more people, but it's already ten past seven."

I used the lull in the conversation to try to do some digging. "How many usually come?"

"Well, turnout is always low, but there are about four regulars, aside from myself. We occasionally have one or two visitors at a time, but most don't come back."

I tried to hide my discomfort. "Why is that?"

The doorbell rang before Carla had the chance to answer. She motioned to me to hold that thought with one finger and rose from the sofa. A moment later, I heard murmured greetings from across the parlor. I picked out a male and female voice that was different from my host. The other woman's tone was friendly and familiar. I suddenly felt like an outsider and wished for a way out.

Carla walked back into the living room with a man and a woman, Phil and Ellie Durst. The best I could guess, they were in their mid to late fifties. Phil had receding salt and pepper hair, round glasses, a sharp nose, and a warm smile. He had a medium to thin build, with a large round belly common for men of his age. Ellie had pin straight black hair, heavy dark makeup that did its best to hide her encroaching age, and piercing dark brown eyes that were nearly black. Her brooding façade contrasted sharply with her soft smile.

I stood and shook both of their hands and offered my name, but not much else. They took a seat on the light green sofa. Carla offered them coffee as well. While she flitted to the kitchen I waited in uncomfortable silence that was more my doing than Phil and Ellie's. They seemed more than willing to engage me, but I did my best to avoid eye contact. It wasn't my intention to be rude, but something about the two of them made me uncomfortable. There was nothing specific I could point to, just an energy that made me uneasy. I crossed my arms and stared at a spot on the coffee table. Ellie leaned forward and smiled at me. I smiled back and took a sip of my coffee.

Carla returned seconds later with three mismatched coffee cups on a silver tray. She set the tray down and offered a mug to Phil and Ellie before taking one herself. She sat down on the brown sofa and grabbed a cheap notebook and pen off the seat beside her. "Thank you for coming out today, Phil, Ellie, and our new friend, Alex. I'm so glad you could make it."

Phil and Ellie smiled and nodded, so polite. I offered a half smile.

Carla opened the notebook and read something to herself, then set it on the coffee table. She turned toward me. "Alex, we usually go around the table and talk about anything that we experienced since the last meeting or anything we want to talk about or explore. We don't limit ourselves just to UFO's, aliens, and extraterrestrials. Anything supernatural is fair game."

"Ok," I said and nodded.

Carla paused for a moment. I hoped she wouldn't ask me to start because that was not going to happen.

"Ellie, why don't we start with you?"

"Sure," Ellie began and leaned forward. "I had the dream again; the one where I'm surrounded by white light and taken up into the sky. Everything goes black and I have no idea what happens next, but I wake up exhausted. My doctor thinks its fatigue or possibly fibromyalgia, but I don't buy it. I think when I have those dreams I'm being abducted. But for what, I have no clue."

Crazy, was the first thought that popped into my mind. Ellie spoke so openly and matter of fact about something so absurd that my senses couldn't help but be offended. I felt doors closing in my mind and wanted nothing more than to get up and walk out of the meeting. But something stopped me. The memory of the bright light flooding the cabin of my truck popped into my brain. I uncrossed my arms and clenched my hands together in front of me.

Carla wrote something in her notebook and took a reflective moment before she spoke. "Interesting. That's the second time this week, Ellie. It seems like this activity is increasing in frequency. Did you see anything Phil?"

"Nothing. I slept like a baby." He gripped Ellie's hand tighter and gave her a look of pity. "Not last night anyway. As you know there have been nights when I have halfway woken up and Ellie was gone out of the bed. When that happens, I never seem to fully awaken and slip back into sleep. When I wake up in the morning she's always there."

Carla picked up the notebook and added something else to it. "Is there anything else?"

Phil and Ellie both shook their heads.

Carla turned her body to face me. I felt a cold sweat forming but resolved to appear calm.

"Alex, I don't expect you to share anything at your very first meeting, but if you did want to share, just let me know."

I shook my head. I wasn't sharing anything with these people.

Carla continued facilitating the meeting. "Ok. I really haven't had anything strange happen to me. As Phil and Ellie know, I love to study this stuff, but I haven't personally experienced anything I could directly claim was supernatural or extraterrestrial. But I do follow a lot of online groups, and it seems like there has been an uptick in UFO sightings and abductions."

My heart skipped a beat and I swallowed hard. That was not what I wanted to hear. I picked up the now lukewarm cup of coffee and took a long drink. My hand trembled as I set the mug down on the coffee table. I remembered the intense darkness of those oval shaped eyes on my drive home the other night.

"Alex, is everything okay?" Carla asked, concerned.

"Yes, I'm fine. I just haven't been feeling that well lately." It was only a partial lie. I really hadn't been myself since I'd seen that spinning disc of lights above my truck.

"I'm sorry. Let me know if you need anything."

I nodded.

Carla continued to talk about the anecdotal increase in supernatural sightings. Phil and Ellie were enraptured. All three of them threw out potential theories for this. Phil wondered if there would be an impending alien invasion. Ellie mentioned that a better general awareness and willingness of witnesses to talk about their experiences contributed to the perception that the activity was on the rise. I tuned most of their chatter out, stuck in my own spinning world. My heart still fought to deny the truth my mind knew plainly. I saw what I saw, and there was no taking back the alien craft that floated above my car, or the creature I'd seen on my way home.

Before giving myself time to think, I blurted out the words I knew I would regret, interrupting Phil, who was in the middle of expounding the details of one of a dozen prevailing theories. "I saw a spaceship, a UFO, about a week ago."

My outburst got everyone's attention.

Carla spoke. "I knew there was a reason you came to us. What happened, Alex?"

I told them everything, including parts I'd left out when I talked with Alicia. I poured my heart out to this group of strangers, vomiting up all the details. I told them all about my fear of seeing things that I had no desire to see. I talked about the weird way Charlie acted when I came home that first night. I recounted the suffocating feeling of being watched in the darkness of my bedroom. I even shared the difficulty of driving home after seeing that creature in the middle of the road on my way home from work.

No one spoke for a few moments after I had finished. I closed my eyes and once again wanted to disappear.

Carla broke the silence with chilling words. "Alex, I have read many cases of alien encounters and the things you have seen and experienced so far have in almost all cases acted as a precursor to a chain of unavoidable events. For lack of a better explanation, seeing a UFO and an alien being within such a short time indicates a sort of preparation for things to come. There is a progression to these events."

She struggled for the right words, hesitating. "I hate to even say this, but you may be looking at a slow crawl toward a close encounter of the fourth kind." She refused to say the word *abduction*.

"Now, that's not always the case. There are some accounts where the supernatural activity stops altogether, but no one really understands why. And in most of the reported cases, the progression is inevitable."

I started to hyperventilate. Ellie's dark eyes went wide as Phil jumped up to help me. The world became dotted with black spots and I felt reality slipping away from me. I gripped the arm of the chair and fought to regain control of my breathing. I gulped at the air, struggling for oxygen. Tears popped up in my eyes. I felt a flood of embarrassment as I realized the spectacle I made of myself.

When I finally calmed down, I spoke with a hoarse voice. My throat felt as raw as my nerves. "What can I do? I don't want to be taken by these things."

Ellie spoke first, and her words cut to the bone. "There's usually nothing you can do but wait, and try to prepare."

I snapped my head up, feeling wild, desperate. "I don't want to prepare. I want to stay right here. How do I stop it from happening?"

Carla spoke with compassion but was unflinching in her delivery of the truth. "How do you stop a bullet once it's left the barrel of a gun?"

I put my head in my hands and groaned. My stomach churned and threatened to spew the coffee, along with the burger and fries I'd eaten earlier, all over the nice carpet. Carla had basically told me that my situation was hopeless and there was nothing I could do to stop what was happening to me. My abduction was imminent. It was my destiny. A fate I must embrace.

The silence in the room was unbearable. There were no comforting lies to reassure me that nothing would happen to me. I waited for someone to offer a potential solution, but no one said a word. There was nothing to say.

Carla ended the meeting early by bringing out a plate of fresh baked chocolate chip cookies. I took one and ate it in almost one bite. It was soft, warm, and tasted amazing, just like the coffee. I'd take what little comfort I could get.

As I left, Carla asked me if I would be coming back on Saturday. I told her there was a greater chance of pigs flying through the eye of a needle that was on fire, which made her laugh, but I could tell she was hurt. It didn't matter. I wasn't going to think about this crap anymore. If I didn't think about it, the next close encounter wouldn't happen. How could it if I was unwilling to entertain the thought? It was flawed logic to be sure, but we all cope by lying to ourselves on occasion.

She handed me a business card with her name and phone number. The silver disc-shaped logo emblazoned across the top of the card complimented the artful design of the Avondale Paranormal Society font. I thanked her for it and for her hospitality, took the card and shoved it in my pocket with no intention of ever using it.

● ● ●

The drive back home after my first meeting with Carla and crew was tense but uneventful. The long trip gave me time to calm down and contemplate what to do next. I decided I'd do just what I'd always done. Going back to my monotonous life was the best way to break free from this trip outside my routine. I would do whatever it took to forget the events of the past few weeks. It was the only way I knew how to keep a tenuous grip on my sanity.

· 7 ·

For the next two weeks, my life carried on. I did not go back to the Avondale Paranormal Society. I saw no strange lights in the sky. There were no odd creatures to greet me on my way to or from work. Charlie acted more or less like himself. I was also back to a state of normal. I worked. I ate. I slept. I pushed down the awful memories and fears of the past month, and could almost allow myself to pretend everything was as it was before. But Carla's words tumbled around in my head, and deep down in those moments when I was really honest with myself, I recognized that there are some things in life that prevent us from ever going back to the way things were.

At work, Alicia had stopped pressing me for information. In fact, she had almost quit talking to me altogether, aside from pleasantries and necessary conversation. She shared enough for me to know that there were some major marital issues at home, and it was hard for her to care about anything but her own problems. I took no offense as it was not personal. There was one thing that was different; Alicia showed up for work on time. John continued to show up late. We both covered for him.

More time passed as late spring transitioned into early summer. The leaves on all the deciduous trees had bloomed into fullness. They hadn't quite gotten past the first green of new growth, but their leaves had all unfolded. The birds and insects had fully returned as well. It was good to see and hear life in action. I was grateful for the distraction from the murky prospects of my own uncertain future.

• • •

I thought of my experience at the Avondale Paranormal Society during my seven o' clock perimeter check of the factory on a Saturday. The meeting would have just started. I wondered what dreams Ellie might have had, or if Carla had heard of any more UFO sightings. I secretly hoped for neither and tried to think about something else.

I took a deep breath and relaxed as I took in my surroundings. The sun was still up in the bright blue western sky emanating warmth and light. White fluff from cottonwood trees blew across the fields on a lazy breeze, dancing through the air to a new home. That same breeze shook the leaves of the forest. I slowed my pace to a casual stroll and felt a tranquil calm seep into my bones.

The drive home that night was uneventful. I no

longer gripped the steering wheel like it was a life preserver, and drove along at a steady pace. To allow the sweet smell of leaves and wet dirt into the truck, I rolled the windows down. The wind rushed through the cabin and I felt invigorated, alive.

That night's sleep was the best I'd had in a long time. If I had any dreams I did not remember them. I woke up refreshed and really took my time getting started for the day. There was no reason to be in a mad rush. I made coffee and drank it from my favorite chipped blue mug in my pajamas and robe on the porch. It was still early enough in the season for the morning to have a little bit of a nip in the air.

The rest of the day passed easily enough. I picked and poked around the house, cleaning and straightening things up here and there. It was late afternoon by the time I took out the riding lawnmower and took my time trimming the large lawn. The smell of fresh cut grass filled my nostrils with its heady, earthy mixture.

As I came to the last section of the yard, I noticed light grey clouds to the west. The weather forecast had called for a chance of rain that afternoon, with the potential for a thunderstorm or two. It was just what my grass needed.

After I finished mowing I drove the lawnmower into the garage and found myself whistling. Next, I checked the yard and scanned the property to make sure I'd moved everything that could get damaged in the rain out of the open air. It was quick work since I hadn't really done much outside yet that season. I hadn't even planted my little vegetable garden and the window of time to do so was closing.

I checked the sky again and the clouds were much darker than they were a moment ago. They also appeared to move a little faster toward my location, and I felt the first chilled breeze of the summer storm. I walked inside, grabbed a lemonade from the fridge, and went right to one of the wooden Adirondack chairs on the covered porch that had been handmade by my father before I was born. It was my favorite place to watch storms come rolling in.

The rain started slow, dropping little spatters here and there. The sound of thunder crashed in the distance. A few moments later the sky brightened with a flash of lightning. I counted the seconds between the flash and the thunder that followed, judging the distance between the heart of the storm and my current location. It was something my grandfather had taught me as a child.

I made it to fifteen seconds before I heard the crack of thunder peel across the forest. Encouraged by the sudden rumble, the rain fell at a steadier pace. I heard the droplets ping off the metal roof on the porch. Another flash of lightning blazed in the distance and I counted again. Twelve seconds. The storm was getting closer.

A bright blue bolt of unharnessed electricity flashed across the sky. I only made it to ten seconds that time. The storm was moving fast. A gust of wind blew under the covered porch causing the ancient wind chimes to play their familiar discordant tune. I hadn't been paying attention to the progress of this particular weather system and had no idea that a tornado watch had been issued for the area.

A twinge of something, perhaps intuition, told me to go inside and turn on the television. As soon as the screen came to life, the emergency broadcast siren preceded a female reporter.

"A tornado has touched down in Forest County

and everyone in the viewing area is urged to take shelter immediately. I repeat. A tornado warning has been issued for all of Forest County."

I stared at the screen, dumbfounded that this storm had found a way to mess up my perfect day. Charlie walked up to me, whimpered, and pushed his head into my hand. He wasn't the kind of dog who was terrified of thunderstorms like some, but he did experience a significant amount of anxiety when the weather became too intense. I patted him on the head as a gust of wind howled through the eaves outside.

The ticker at the bottom of the screen ran through the rest of the counties in the area under a severe thunderstorm warning followed by those under a tornado watch. Forest County was on both lists as well as the only one with a tornado warning. The rain hit harder on the roof, marking time with its own wild beat.

I should have heeded the advice to seek shelter and head to the basement. Instead, I turned up the volume on the television and walked back to the front porch. I left the door open so that I could hear more specific information about the storm. The rain came down heavy and puddles formed in the recesses of the yard. It was the first significant rainfall of the summer. The farmers would be thrilled. Early summer rain was a major predictor of the potential for an abundant harvest. Thunder cracked in the clouds.

A rush of cold wind swept under the porch roof and chilled me to the bone. I shivered as I stepped closer toward the yard. The sky brightened to a sickly shade of yellow. I walked onto the steps and looked up. Clouds so dark they were almost black raced across the sky. Another bright blue bolt of lightning zig-zagged into the forest just a few miles away. I retreated up the steps.

The yellow hue changed to green, and I heard what sounded like little stones smacking against the steel roof. I watched flecks of white roll off the roof and bounce on the ground. It was hail. In seconds, the ground was covered in a blanket of the icy pellets. If it kept up much longer the fate of those young crops that needed the rain would turn, and they would be destroyed by the hailstorm.

The little balls of ice grew bigger, changing from pea to acorn to golf ball size. I remained transfixed by the phenomenon as I heard loud clunking on the roof followed by orange-sized hail rolling into the yard. I backed away from the edge of the porch and into the house. I shut the front door, but could not close out the sound of the large hail as it beat against the house.

The emergency siren blared from the television, barely audible above the onslaught. The meteorologist pointed to a weather map of the state. A tornado had touched down in Arlen County, which was to the immediate west of Forest County. The weather reporter called it an F3, not the strongest of twisters, but one that could put a serious dent in your day.

I watched as the graphic showed the whirlwind move from Arlen to Forest County. The rectangular shape of my home county on the screen was highlighted in red. Charlie came up behind me, running in circles and whimpering. I had to get to the basement. A rush of wind battered the western side of the house, along with the rat-a-tat-tat sound of hail. The sound of shattering glass came from my sister's old room.

Severe storms were a regular occurrence in that part of the country, but tornadoes of any kind were rare. I whistled for Charlie, who was already at my side. We both scrambled out of the living room and ran to the basement door. The sounds of rain, hail, and harsh bursts of wind slamming against the house were all around us.

Charlie bolted down the stairs as soon as I opened the door. He padded to the bottom and sat down there, whining for me to join him, pleading with his puppy dog eyes. I was just about to go down when I realized I had no flashlight, candle, or even a lighter. It was daytime and there were small block windows for light, but if the power went out it would be plenty gloomy down there.

A loud crash from outside forced me to abandon my search. I flipped the switch at the top of the steps to turn on the bare light bulbs that hung from the ceiling downstairs and shut the door hard behind me. Once I reached the bottom, Charlie followed me to the southwest corner of the basement. It was the corner that was supposed to be the safest if a twister was bearing down. Or maybe it was the southeast. I stayed where I was, hoping it was the right choice.

One of the small glass windows to my right imploded and glass skittered across the cement floor. Charlie whimpered. I knelt down and held him tight to my side. The wind blew through the now open window and created a low whistling sound that changed in tone with the intensity of the air that rushed through it.

Within seconds of the window shattering a sound like a freight train filled the room. I know people have used the same analogy to describe the sound of a tornado, but there is really nothing like hearing it to know how true that description is. I closed my eyes and gripped my dog tighter, bracing for the worst. The lights flickered but remained lit.

I heard the buzz crack of the power fighting the urge to fail when I realized the wind, hail, and rain had decreased. A bright flash and clap of thunder reminded me of the big show in the sky was still going on, but the brunt of the storm seemed to have passed. I dared to open my eyes.

The lights brightened before returning to an intermittent state of brownout. They were still buzzing when I led Charlie out of the basement. The reporter on the local news channel was still doing her job from the studio far away from danger. Pictures of the devastation caused by the storm flashed on the screen. The side of one house was peeled back, revealing the ruined furniture and belongings within. Several mobile homes had found new places to land, one flipped completely upside down. In all of these pictures, the victims of this cruel trick of nature were soaked and dirty, burnt out shells of their former selves shuffling through the debris of their lives.

I walked past the living room toward the room where I heard the sound of breaking glass. It was the second door on the left, the one that used to be my sister's room. The top pane of the window facing the yard had been blasted by hail. The half melted ball of ice sat on the hardwood floor, surrounded by glittering glass. The gauzy curtain billowed in the breeze.

I walked out of the room and put on my work boots to look for additional damage outside. Other than the windows in my sister's room and the basement, the house seemed to be in good shape. Some debris had blown into the yard, but nothing serious. I'd have to get on the roof later to check for warped or damaged panels. The roof over the porch was intact, albeit with a few more dents than before.

While I escaped the brunt of the storm, I couldn't help but think how that pleasant day had turned into a nightmare. I stared in wonder at a fifty-yard-wide swath of churned up earth about five hundred yards away from the house. It cut a path from across the road into the forest at the other side of my property line. The grass and overgrown vegetation of the neglected farmland in the damage zone was gone, replaced by swirled patches of dirt. The tornado had come so close to the house. Too close. There was no amount of nurturing or reasoning that could sway the forces of nature, but something spared the house.

The storm had destroyed my attempt to experience a peaceful day at home. The trembling I had not felt for several weeks returned. The storm could have killed me and Charlie, and I had stood outside like a moron, watching as it approached. The sudden storm served as a reminder that by attempting to move on with my life I was doing nothing more than ignoring the immediate danger ahead of me. No amount of pretending could make the monster not real. I suppose I knew that all along, but the truth hit me hard at that moment.

The sun had just slipped past the tree line as I hammered the last nail in a piece of plywood I put up to temporarily block the broken window in my sister's old bedroom. I'd get a replacement pane, and call the insurance company, but the deductible was likely to exceed the cost of any repairs due to the storm damage. I'd have to pay for a new window out of pocket.

I was able to replace the basement window as I had a few spares lying around that my father picked up from a neighbor before he died. I thought about giving them away a number of times, but who knew that all these years later my decision to hold onto them would have paid off. I wondered what else might have come in handy that I trashed when both my parents passed away. After I finished in the basement I went back outside to do a final sweep of the property before full dark took hold. I walked around the house, making sure I hadn't missed anything that needed immediate attention. Charlie trailed along behind me, sniffing in the dirt. I'd have to clean up some of the debris in the yard a bit, but the biggest part of the job was done.

A warm and gentle breeze carried the scent of earth, leaves, and the freshness that only a rainstorm can bring. I took a deep breath, filling my lungs with the rejuvenated air. I looked up and the clouds had all blown away, leaving a crystal clear sky. There was no moon and the stars shone with unbridled brilliance. Each one twinkled as I'd never seen them before.

I stopped and stood in the backyard to get a better view. The vastness of space left me in awe. It felt like the first time I'd gazed at the stars and pondered the distant galaxies beyond our own. I was reminded of a balmy summer night when I camped out in the backyard with my sister to watch a meteor shower. The streaks of burning white light were more infrequent than I had imagined, but when they blazed across the sky it was magical.

The star shine reflected dully off the lawn. Charlie strolled over to where I stood, walked in a circle, and laid down in the grass, letting out a humph. The nice memories of my childhood were interrupted by more recent thoughts of the things I'd seen just a handful of weeks ago. The starlight suddenly seemed too bright, threatening somehow. Each twinkling pulse seemed to draw the burning balls of gas closer. I had the irrational fleeting thought that the stars would fall toward the earth, sealing the collective doom of the planet. The walls of the infinite universe beyond closed in on me. I found it difficult to breathe.

I stared into the darkness dotted with pulsing starlight and trembled at the sheer immensity of the universe. The endless possibilities of other worlds and beings superior to those here on earth crept into my brain. From galaxies far away, our little blue planet was nothing more than a blip, if it was even visible at all. And it was quite possible I'd had an encounter with a being from one of those distant places.

My rational mind fought against the idea of explorers from other planets, but my gut reminded me of the truth. I'd seen a spaceship hovering over my truck that night that felt so long ago. I'd also seen one of its passengers on the side of the road like some monstrous hitchhiker from hell. I remembered those eyes, those endless pools of blackness. The knowledge of the stars that burned above me was in those eyes; the knowledge of worlds millions of light years away. I wrapped my arms around myself and knelt down on the lawn. I wept hot, bitter tears. The storm had shaken me out of my cocoon of comfort and denial. The night sky reminded me what I was up against.

● ● ●

I'm not sure how long I was out there in the grass crying over the acceptance of my fate, but it was a long time. Charlie stayed with me, ever my faithful companion and friend. I was exhausted from the emotional turmoil of processing this thing that did not seem rational and that I did not want to believe. My self-imposed loneliness seemed like a bad idea for the first time. My only connections to the outside world were my co-worker Alicia and the kooks at the Avondale Paranormal Society. I groaned as I pulled myself up off the ground. I knew I'd see Carla again.

I slept fitfully that night. My dreams were plagued by the spinning lights of the UFO, the beam of bright white light, and the awful little creature whose mere gaze had the ability to penetrate the depths of my soul. Throughout the night, my mind struggled and failed to work out a solution to my dark fate. The only thing left was to embrace it and learn as much as I could about the experience before they came for me.

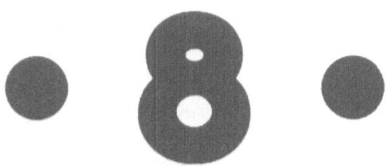

More time passed and my life carried on as it had before. There was a marked difference between my thinking before and after the storm. I was no longer able to deny that I had no control over the future. Survival and hoping I'd be skipped over were my only goals. Carla's words at the only Avondale Paranormal Society meeting I attended rang through my mind. Consecutive close encounters are progressive, culminating in the fourth kind, abduction. I was a marked man.

Alicia noticed the change in my behavior and tried to draw the reason out of me. I made up some story about missing my sister, which was partially true, but not the real reason. She accepted my explanation on the surface, but I could tell from her sideways glances and the unspoken questions evident in her facial expressions that she knew something else was going on with me. I refused to share anything with her, or anyone else. After a few days of persistent questioning, she dropped the issue. Her relationship with her husband was getting worse. She had her own life to worry about.

It was a Wednesday afternoon, my regular day off when I nearly broke down and called Carla. I'd kept her business card in my wallet this whole time, I suppose as a sort of lifeline, my last resort when everything else I tried had failed.

In order to trick myself into ignorance, I refused to research anything about UFO's, aliens, or abductions. Knowledge is power in many of life's circumstances, but knowledge combined with the inability to alter a situation is nothing more than torture. I've done plenty of research since that time in my life, but nothing I would have learned at that point would have prepared me for the experience or guided me down the path to the truth I discovered later.

I turned the business card over in my hands and traced the flying saucer logo. Instead of finding my phone and calling Carla, I put the card back in my wallet. I had other things to do, like grocery shopping. I was out of everything. Even poor Charlie had suffered for days with nothing but kibble. I set my wallet on the counter next to my keys and cell phone.

I was showered and dressed by early afternoon, after spending much of the day loafing around the house. I wrote a vague grocery list, but since I needed almost everything I didn't bother making it too long. Anything I forgot I could pick up at the Big River Gas Station.

The drive to Avondale was quiet and the temperature was warm, but not uncomfortable. I rolled the window down and let the fresh air swirl around the cabin. I almost felt carefree as the wind caressed my skin. White puffy clouds floated lazily through the sky.

Some people gather their groceries by shopping

multiple stores with loads of coupons, discount cards, and circulars with the specials highlighted to maximize their savings. These extreme deal seekers inconvenience themselves with the loss of countless hours for a savings of a few bucks. I was not and am not one of those people. I prefer to shop at one or two stores with reasonable prices, and seek the lower priced items in the store, but I never spend much time obsessing about it.

I pulled into the parking lot at the Wal-Mart that was the source of much controversy in the community. It took years of town hall meetings and empty promises before it was finally built. All the protests and complaining did nothing to stop it. I found a spot near the exit door and parked the truck between the lines almost perfectly.

About an hour later, I emerged from the store with the spoils of my own personal shopping war. I spent a bit of time in the back of the truck, separating my items by those that needed refrigeration and those that did not. Living so far away from town, I bought a large electric cooler to use specifically for trips to the grocery store. It was large enough to hold all of my cold and frozen food, and then some. I also used the cooler when I went camping with Charlie a couple of times.

After sorting and securing the groceries, I closed the liftgate, climbed into the truck, and worked my way toward the exit of the parking lot. Without thinking, I merged into the right turn lane. Going right would take me further into town. I had no intention of running any other errands, but my gut insisted I turn right. The rational part of me wanted to fight the urge, but I followed my instinct.

A short time later I found myself parked in front of Carla's house. I had no conscious desire to be there, but my subconscious had worked hard to tell me where to go. I knew I needed help, and if I was too afraid to ask for it, the deepest part of myself would do it for me. I shut off the engine and sat in the truck, wrestling with the decision to go knock on her door.

I decided it would be best to let this particular experience play itself out and learn what I could from it. Carla possessed knowledge and insight into the supernatural that I did not. She had studied the subject for decades and met countless numbers of people who had seen things most people never see. The things I had seen. I got out of the truck.

There was still three hours until the Avondale Paranormal Society meeting, but I needed to speak with Carla now. Maybe this was my chance to see her outside of the meeting, to discover how she acted apart from the environment where I'd first met her. I put my hands in the pockets of my well-worn jeans and walked slow toward her house. I couldn't remember if she held down a job aside from her self-professed paranormal investigator role and half-hoped that she wouldn't be there.

By the time I reached the door, I knew she was home. The smell of fresh baked cookies and singing gave her away. I took a deep breath and rang the bell. The singing stopped. I heard her footsteps as she walked toward me. The curtain on the small window to the side of the door parted, and the lock on the door unlatched.

Carla had a genuine look of shock on her face as the door swung open. Her white hair was as wild as ever, and she wore a teal apron covered in white flour. "Why Alex, what a nice surprise. I wasn't sure if I'd ever see you again. Please come in."

I hesitated a moment before accepting her

invitation, as though she was the one who dropped in on me unexpected. I gave her an awkward half smile and stepped inside. Carla closed the door behind me and grabbed my hand. "Come into the kitchen with me. I need to keep an eye on these cookies. The timing on those darn things can be so sensitive."

I followed her in silence.

As I sat down at the small black metal table in the kitchen, Carla offered me some coffee and I accepted, grateful for the distraction. She handed me a mug that smelled like heaven and sat down across from me, an inquisitive look on her face. I took a sip and closed my eyes. The coffee was just as good as the last time I'd had it.

She pushed aside her own steaming cup and leaned back, a quirky smile on her face. "What is it that brings you here, Alex? The meeting isn't for a few hours."

My heart pounded. "I...I need some advice. I've really been struggling since the meeting. I've tried to avoid thinking about everything that happened to me, but it won't stop haunting me." I tried to fight back the tears that came fast and hot. "I'm scared, Carla. I'm just so scared."

The usual glint of mischievous curiosity in her eyes was replaced with empathy. She reached out and grabbed my hands in both of hers. "Oh Alex, please don't be scared. Whoever these visitors are, they mean you no harm. From what I have seen, they only intend to study us, to learn more about us. I have to believe they have no intention of hurting us."

I pulled my hands away and looked at her. "What about the women who claim to have been impregnated by aliens, or those who claim to have been probed...you know...anally?"

117

Carla waved me off and chuckled. "Those are sensationalist stories told by crackpots and conspiracy theorists. Most people I have talked to hardly remember anything about their abduction."

I became incredulous. "How can you possibly know that those people who don't remember just chose to block out their memories?"

Her wild eyes flashed with indignation. "I don't know that for sure, but I have spent most of my life studying these things and in all of that work I have never proven that they intend to do anything more than study us. It's like a scientist on earth studying a mouse."

"And that doesn't worry you? I can think of some pretty awful things people have done to mice in the name of science."

Carla huffed at me, annoyed by where the conversation was headed. "Well, one major difference is that everyone who has been abducted by aliens has come back to tell the tale. Mice are rarely that lucky."

I crossed my arms, skeptical of her naïve explanation. I wondered if she was being genuine or just playing dumb. "Of course only the people who came back shared their stories. How could someone who never returned tell you about being abducted? What about the people who go missing every day and nobody ever sees them again?"

She pushed her chair away from the table, agitated. The sound of the wood scraping against the hard tile set off a nerve in my molars. She stormed away, muttering something to herself that I could not understand. I sat at the table contemplating my next move.

After a few seconds, I went in search of Carla. I felt bad for pushing her to the point of having to leave the room and wanted to apologize for causing any offense. But the truth was that hurting her feelings did not invalidate my point. How could anyone know for certain how many people abducted by aliens simply vanished, never to be heard from again? And even if some crackpot had seen a spaceship or an alien creature and then disappeared, who would think to connect the dots? I started to wish I'd never thought of the possibility as I contemplated my own fate.

I found Carla sitting on the living room sofa hunched over a notebook. She flipped through the pages with such force that I was sure she would rip them from the metal spiral holding them together. I waited in the entryway for her to notice my presence.

She slammed the notebook closed, let out an exasperated sigh, and pushed it off her lap onto the floor. The pages fluttered as it flew through the air. When she turned to look up at me, her face was twisted with pain and confusion. "Why did you have to bring up the people that have disappeared, Alex? Why?"

I stood there shocked, not knowing the right thing to say. "It's just something that came to mind. Just a random, disturbing thought. I had no idea it would upset you so much. Your reaction is scaring me more than the question, Carla. What's going on?"

There are some questions that I wish I'd never asked and that was one of them.

Carla turned to look at me, her face red and tears forming in the corner of her right eye. "Alex, I think it's best if you sit down for this."

"I think I'll stand, thank you very much. Just tell me what you know." I leaned against the doorway and crossed my arms. There was no way I was sitting down for this.

She huffed again. "Suit yourself. I guarantee you'll be sitting soon enough."

I shifted from one foot to the other, encouraging her to speak with what I hoped was an intimidating stare.

"I was twenty-two years old when my husband was abducted and disappeared."

That got my attention. I had no words to convey my reaction as I staggered over to the nearest chair and fell into it. Carla continued.

"Dick and I were married for just over a year and a half when it happened. He'd been raving for months about seeing UFO's and dreaming about being abducted. I wanted so much to deny that he was telling the truth, to pretend he was just having a mental breakdown or something. I refused to listen to him. One night, we went to bed as usual, and when I woke up he was gone. No note, nothing disturbed. But that wasn't the strangest part."

"The boxer shorts and t-shirt he'd worn to bed that night were still there on his side of the bed. It was as if he'd slid out of his clothes without ever disturbing them. I had no explanation. The primary detective assigned to the case assured me I was off my rocker when I told him what Dick had been telling me for months. His theory was that my husband had simply taken off on me, but I knew the truth. Dick had been going on and on about how he was going to be taken away by aliens and never return. I never expected it to actually happen. I never thought in a million years that it could be true." She put her face in her hands and sobbed.

"Oh my..." Those were the only words I could utter. My mind folded in on itself in a feeble attempt to protect what was left of my sanity.

Carla lifted her face and locked her eyes with

mine. "I've spent nearly four decades searching for evidence that whatever is behind these abductions is simply curious about humans, and at most benign entities that mean us no harm. Aside from my husband and one other woman who had similar dreams, but was never actually abducted, you are the only one who has challenged my hope-filled assertions about the intentions of these creatures. I wanted so badly to believe their intentions were altruistic. Thinking anything else is unbearable. "

The self-proclaimed expert being schooled by me – the green under the gills student – made me want to bolt from the room. If she doubted their intentions, what did that mean for me? Instead of running, I asked another stupid question (and yes, there are stupid questions). "Has anyone been abducted and returned…later?"

Carla gave a little laugh and covered her mouth with her hand, stifling its impact. "Oh yes. There have been those who claim to have been taken and returned days, weeks, months, or years after being abducted, but the vast majority of those individuals have one thing in common. When they come back, they are shells of their former selves. Most are diagnosed with PTSD or some other mental disorder and are incapable of carrying on a normal life. Before the age of psychological enlightenment, many of these people were locked up in mental hospitals and subjected to further torture from their doctors. They were prime candidates for lobotomies and electroshock therapy. But let me be crystal clear with you. Despite the mental acrobatics of my self-denial for the sake of my lost husband, no one returns unchanged. Not even those who are taken and returned the same night."

The plush seat I sat in became uncomfortable. I

shifted and readjusted, but could not shake the awful feeling forming in the pit of my stomach that swirled up my spine. From everything she had told me since the first time I'd met her I was a marked man, destined for abduction. I felt the stress of the situation bear down on my brain, stretching the limits of my mental endurance.

Carla could tell I was lost in my thoughts. She tried to offer me some words of encouragement. "If it helps, those people who are missing for long stretches of time are exceedingly rare. Many of them, after recovering from the experience, are thrilled at having been used to further the understanding of the human race. And there's always the chance that you failed their pre-testing, that nothing will come of this at all."

As much as I wanted to cling to that hope, I knew it was just a bunch of smoke. The moment that little monster looked into my soul through the rearview mirror of my truck I knew that I was a wanted man. Just how far I would be taken into the corridors of that particular hell had yet to be seen.

I left Carla's house after that. I had no desire to hang around for the fast approaching meeting of the Avondale Paranormal Society.

• • •

That night I dreamed of standing in an open field, naked and cold. I was afraid of something that had chased me to this place. I looked all around me, frantic to find something at the edges of the clearing. I felt the rumble of a low hum before I heard it. The wind rustled the trees, and off in the distance I saw a disc of spinning lights. I stifled a scream.

I ran in the opposite direction, hoping to take cover in the trees. As I got closer there was a wall little grey life forms. They locked arms and stared at me with those unblinking black eyes. I stopped short of breaking through their barricade. I might have been able to take one or two of them, but if they all ganged up on me I'd be overpowered.

I weighed my options, but nothing I considered would end in anything but capture. With a willing surrender, I might receive some measure of mercy. But if I fought, I would be forced to do whatever they wanted to do to me anyway.

Defeated, I fell down to my knees and accepted my fate. The UFO crested the tree line on the other side of the clearing and traveled slow toward me. As the alien craft closed to within fifty yards of me a bright beam of light burst to life. I lowered my head and wept.

I felt the coldness of the light before I saw it. When I opened my eyes the light was all around me, enveloping me in its clinical glare. I looked up, and faces lined the ridge of a hole in the bottom of the ship. Dozens of dark eyes stared at me, searching the depths of my soul.

I tried to run, but could not move. I couldn't even blink. By the time I realized my body was floating up into the light there was nothing I could do. The scream I felt inside my mind was unable to form in my throat. A tear streamed down my face.

I woke up drenched in a cold sweat and hyperventilating. Charlie barked at me and backed away into a corner of the room. It was hard to catch a breath and I am sure my poor dog got the scare of his life. I reached over to the left and fell to the floor hard. I crawled my way to the bedroom door, struggling to get out of the room.

I collapsed by the time I reached the door. The lack of oxygen to my brain caused me to pass out. It must have been hours by the time I regained consciousness. I trembled, knowing that the dream was not just a dream, but a taste of things to come. Things I wanted no part of but was powerless to avoid.

• 9 •

everal weeks passed and nothing changed. I drifted through life in cycles of working, sleeping, eating, and cleaning; all things that had previously been enough to keep me going on with my life. An unsatisfied restlessness stirred in my spirit. I longed for the days when I simply existed and didn't think about the inevitable close encounter. I ached for the days when I did not peek around every corner expecting one of those little grey creatures to freeze me in place with its condemning stare.

On one particularly hot and sticky day, I poured a glass of warm sun brewed tea and walked out to the front porch. Heat and humidity are quite possibly the two worst combinations of weather conditions, with the possible exception of a dry and bone-chilling cold. A light breeze passed through the field, a weak whisper of air unable to deliver on its promise of coolness. The heat would not relent for hours, until the sun decided it was time to stop baking the already scorched earth.

"I swear to God Charlie, it must be over a hundred degrees out here." I actually said those words out loud to my dog, not expecting a response, but the words needed to be said.

The old German Shepherd lifted his head off the wood boards of the porch beneath him and gave me a little tilt of his head like he misunderstood me. He knew what I was talking about. I sat down in one of the Adirondack chairs.

That dog day of summer was two months early. Days like those were usually reserved for the middle of July to the middle of August, not middle to late June. I guessed that a good many other people thought so as well. At least the sudden heat would account for the transformer down in Big River blowing out again. Everyone turning on their air conditioners at the same time overloaded the system. I shuddered to think about how fragile our power grid actually was if a few more devices than usual could blow it out.

No one would get any relief until the utility trucks came rumbling to the rescue. Until then, we just had to do what our fathers did before us. Endure. That's a word not used too often these days, but there was a time when all people had to cling to was the hope that endurance brings through suffering. Go through bad enough times, even a boring day seems like a blessing.

I had just started ruminating in the vinegar of my own thoughts when the phone rang. It took great effort to drag myself out of the chair and go back into the house. Sweat poured out of me. With no way to stop the flow, the only thing I could do was try to drink enough liquids to keep up with the loss of fluid. The phone rang again.

The screen door snapped shut behind me and I

walked toward the kitchen. I spotted the phone on the kitchen counter and picked up my pace. It was still blaring its mechanical tune by the time I reached it. I swiped the screen to answer it and put the phone against my sweat-slicked head.

"Hello?"

"Yeah Alex, it's Carla. You got a minute?"

Why was she calling me? My gut told me it was something bad. I shifted my weight from one foot to the other. "I sure do. That is assuming I don't melt first."

"Very funny."

Her tone told me this was not a casual call.

"Anyway, I was doing some research on your old farm out there and found something very interesting. Are you familiar with the name Charles Mayfield?"

I felt like I'd been punched in the stomach. It was a name I knew well. I should have said something at that point, but it was hard to speak.

"Alex, are you there?"

"Yes," I said, breathless. My head was spinning. "Charles Mayfield is my grandfather."

"I was afraid of that. Alex, how much do you know about your grandfather?"

"Not much", I lied. I knew more than I was willing to tell Carla.

"I have a letter here from a woman I presume to be his sister or his wife and some other notes that I think you need to see. Can you meet me somewhere?"

My mouth felt dry. I had no idea what information that mysterious letter and random notes could hold. I knew the story of my grandfather very well. At least the version that had been shared with me. While thinking of an answer to Carla's invitation, I recalled the narrative that had been shared with me my whole life and saw some disconcerting similarities between my grandfather and me. Both of us were loners, and at least one of us was insane. Maybe we both were.

I answered before she wondered if I'd dropped off the face of the earth. "Absolutely. Where do you want to meet?"

"How about Shelby's on the outskirts of town?"

"I'll be there in forty-five minutes."

"Great. I'll see you then."

● ● ●

I hung up the phone and raced to the bathroom. I showered in a hurry and threw on a pair of shorts, a t-shirt, and sandals. With just enough time to make it to the restaurant, I snatched the keys off the hook in the kitchen, shoved my phone and wallet in my pockets, and rushed to the truck. A cloud of dust followed me out of the driveway and onto the blacktop as I sped down the two-lane road with the windows wide open. The hot, humid air blew around me, but I was beyond noticing something so trivial as the temperature. My skin prickled with goosebumps.

My grandfather had been institutionalized for twenty years or so by the time I was born. It was another twenty before he *finally* died. That was how my father always talked about his death. He was *finally* dead. The Lord *finally* took him. It was as if he couldn't wait to wash the stain of the curse of his father's craziness off himself and the rest of the family.

The story was similar to others who've experienced relatives with mental illness. Grandpa Charles started out like most other people, with maybe just a few loose bolts in his brain. He'd forget things, or talk about seeing strange things in the sky. Then he would turn and talk to a flower and get mad when it refused to respond to him. Not all days were like this, but there were enough bad days to cause his wife and children to be wary of his erratic behavior.

My father remembered and repeated some very detailed information about the day the worm turned and my grandfather lost his grip on sanity. After dinner one night, he'd wandered past my grandmother and muttered something about buried varmints. He grabbed the shovel off the stoop and went into the backyard and started digging holes looking for the imaginary vermin. My Grandma Sarah made sure my dad and uncle stayed inside the house for safety, but kept the door open so she could keep an eye on her husband.

She must have turned around and taken her eyes off of him for just a few seconds to put some dishes in the sink. When she looked back through the door her husband had stripped off all his clothes and was cavorting around the backyard, waving the shovel back and forth above his head and screaming. He was a wild man. Most of what he said was unintelligible, but some of it came out sounding like the ravings of a lunatic.

"You're not gonna get me," he screamed and tore at his face, causing the skin to break. Blood ran down his cheeks.

The look of horror and shame on my grandmother's face was enough to make a grown man cry. Or so my father told me. The two little boys kept inside lost much of their innocence that day.

My grandmother was still holding a cast iron pan she intended to carry over to the sink to wash. In shock, she dropped it and the heavy pan clattered to the floor, cracking a tile.

Grandpa Charles turned his head toward the open door. His wild eyes glinted with darkness and reflected the weak moonlight. His expression was feral, more animal than human. He raised the shovel above his head and charged toward the house. Grandma reacted faster than she would have thought possible as she slammed the door shut and locked it. The heavy thud of her husband colliding with the other side of the door confirmed she had made the right decision to shut him out.

She and her boys rushed to lock the front door, side door, and any open windows on the first floor. Charles let out a primal scream, unlike anything they'd ever heard. He ran around the outside of the house, naked as the day he was born and pounded on windows as he tried to find a way inside.

Sarah was scared like she had never been before, but tried to hide it from her children. Shaking, she walked into the kitchen and made the call she dreaded. Her hand trembled as she dialed the number for the Forest County Sheriff's Department. A moment later, an operator answered the phone. No longer able to hold back her emotions, my grandmother burst into tears.

Charles Mayfield was picked up by the police that day and committed into a psychiatric hospital for the rest of his life. Sarah attempted to visit him often in the beginning, but he was incapable of relating to other human beings. He had become an unrecognizable savage beyond all hope of salvation.

The thought of the same thing happening to me terrified me to the core.

• • •

I focused on the road ahead of me, but my mind was miles away. My gut told me that the information Carla had about my grandfather was somehow related to what was happening to me. And I was not going to like it. The familiar feeling of despair swept through me. Why was I even bothering to meet her when I knew she was going to doom me to the same fate?

Shelby's Restaurant came into view. When it first opened, Shelby's was a nice family restaurant that enjoyed a decent amount of business. That was before the chains took over and everyone abandoned the local flavor. As the years passed, the owner, Tom Shelby, found it harder and harder to just break even. As a result of the lack of available funds, combined with a gambling habit that refused to subside despite his dwindling funds, Mr. Shelby had allowed the place to fall into all sorts of disrepair. The roof was in bad shape. The paint had long since faded, chipped, and peeled away. The once brightly lit letters that spelled out Shelby's were badly faded, and when the lights came on at night it spelled "elb's". As a result, it became a greasy spoon frequented primarily by old-time locals who wanted nothing more than a cheap bite to eat and to avoid the rest of the world.

I pulled into the mostly dirt lot and parked next to Carla's car. She drove a newer model mid-sized Toyota. Like everything else about her, it was modest and sensible. No one looking at Carla or her car would guess that she was an expert in UFOs and alien abductions. Unless of course, they asked her about it. Then she was full of all sorts of surprises.

Shelby's wasn't the kind of place where you walked through the doors and waited to be seated by a smiling hostess. It was self-seating and sometimes self-serving, depending on who was working.

The little bell rang as I walked through the door and no one turned to see who had just entered. There was no one who cared enough to notice. The smell of years of soaked-in frying grease assaulted me. It was an aroma I'd grown used to from the years of my youth when my parents took my sister and me out for dinner at Shelby's in its heyday. That was back when eating in a restaurant was a luxury. It was a long time from those days when my biggest concern was deciding between a strawberry or chocolate shake.

I searched the seating area and Carla's shock of frizzy, blond hair caught my eye. I waved to her and a smile lit up her face. She had chosen a booth where we could have a little privacy, not that anyone would pay us much attention. I rushed over to her, both eager to hear what she had to share, and wishing our meeting was over.

Set on the table in front of her were a couple of books, some old notepads, and random papers. My stomach clenched, both at the thought of what she had to share with me and of what the questionable food might do to my digestive system.

It took me a moment to realize that it was a bit chilly inside. I'd grown so used to the heat and humidity on the drive over that I forgot what it felt like to experience a normal temperature. I sat in the booth across from Carla and did my best to put my stone face on. If I looked emotionally impenetrable, maybe I would be.

Carla smiled, and something about the way her lip curled came off like a sneer, serpentine somehow. I brushed the impression aside. She had never been anything but nice to me.

"Alex, thank you for coming to meet me. I know this must sound strange, but I was looking over some old notes and case studies when I ran across the case of Charles Mayfield. It made me think of you immediately."

My intestines clenched again, the pain digging into my lower abdomen. I wondered how I would get through this conversation without having to run to the bathroom. I nodded, encouraging her to continue.

"Mr. Mayfield, it seems, was quite interested in aliens and UFOs at one time. He claimed to have seen an alien spacecraft at nearly the same section of road that you did. His description of the event is almost identical. Here, take a look for yourself."

Carla passed over an open notebook and pointed to a section where my grandfather detailed what he had seen. His handwriting was simple but easy to read, and his description was an almost exact replica of what I had seen that night when my truck died. The sense of Déjà vu was overpowering. He described a bright spotlight, followed by the spinning lights on the bottom of a metal disc, accompanied by a strange hum. The notebook felt hot in my hands. I snapped it shut and thrust it back toward Carla.

"What good does this do me? I already know they're coming for me. Do I have a life of insanity to look forward to as well?"

She gave me a measured look before continuing. "That's not all there is to the story, Alex. There are two more accounts in separate notes. Charles was interviewed two more times by a former colleague of mine before he was too far gone to make any rational sense at all."

Any last vapor of hope I had of denying my fate evaporated. I spit the words out before Carla could speak them. "The same things that are happening to me happened to my grandpa, didn't they?"

"I'm afraid so." She looked pensive, as though she really cared about what I was going through.

My mouth felt dry, but I spoke again. "There's some sort of pattern here. Like a family curse or something, right?"

Carla's eyes brightened. "No, Alex. That's where you're wrong. You and your grandfather were chosen, not cursed. There must be something special about your bloodline that these aliens are interested in."

Her crazed stare made me uncomfortable. I looked around to make sure no one overheard our conversation. "There's nothing special about me or my family."

"But that's where you are wrong. These things don't choose people randomly. You were selected for a specific purpose, a higher purpose."

I shifted on the plastic bench seat and leaned forward. "All my grandfather got out of all that special attention was a life sentence in the nuthouse. I don't want that for myself, Carla."

I slid over to the edge of the booth and made a move to stand. Carla stood up and put a hand on my arm to stop me from leaving. I paused out of respect for all she had done for me up to that point.

"That doesn't have to happen to you. It really doesn't. Not everyone has the same experience. Not everyone is destined for a life of solitude and confinement. Why, many of the people I have spoken to lead very normal lives. More enlightened, perhaps, but normal all the same."

I shrugged away from her grip, my respect at its end. Panic bloomed in my chest and I had to get out of there fast. As I walked through the restaurant toward the front doors, I heard Carla following behind me, pleading with me to stay. I refused to be her pet project.

My pace was fast, but not rushed as I marched toward my truck. I could still hear Carla in the background begging me to let her finish, but I blocked out any words that made any kind of sense. I climbed into my truck, started it up, and drove away from her without looking back. It was only when I was out onto the blacktop that I dared a peek into the rearview mirror. Carla stood in the parking lot behind me, exasperated and defeated. She threw her hands up in the air and turned around, kicking dirt as she walked away. I looked back to the road ahead of me and felt no regret at running away from her.

CLOSER
ENCOUNTERS

• 10 •

The heat did not relent. When I wasn't sleepwalking through work, I was obsessing about my grandfather. I actually bought a laptop, had internet hooked up at my house, and began researching alien abductions and UFO sightings. I could no longer deny the path I was destined to walk, or to be more accurate, had been forced on me. Either way, it didn't matter. I figured I might as well learn as much as I could about the phenomenon.

My faithful dog Charlie made attempts to comfort me. He'd force me to pet him and tried to appeal to me with his toys, but all his efforts came to nothing. I pet him out of obligation, threw a ball with half a heart once in a while. He could tell I wasn't engaged. Each day that passed, a little bit more of the person I knew slipped away. I was becoming someone else altogether; someone with a purpose. When I wasn't ignoring Charlie, I spent my time tending to my physical needs and fed my compulsion to learn more about my fate.

The question I asked did not have an answer. I wanted to know why I was chosen. Why me and not some other unlucky schlub? All I could think was that somewhere down the line, a branch on the family tree had done something so bad that a stain was left on future generations. I was just the next in line to inherit the family curse.

It was strange to be comforted by the fact that there were so many people from all walks of life, all over the world, who could relate to my situation. They were people I would never meet, but we shared a connection. One thing I learned from all that research that might have helped me was the similarity of the abduction experiences. I started to think I knew what to expect.

The clock struck 4:00 a.m. when I decided I'd had enough of spider-webbing through the internet and closed the top of my shiny new laptop. When I stood from the chair, Charlie rose from where he lay under the kitchen table and followed me across the living room and up the stairs. While I made a pit stop at the bathroom, he sauntered into the bedroom to make himself comfortable.

A few minutes later, I joined him. As I told you before, Charlie had his bed on the floor, but every night since I saw that thing on the road in the rearview mirror, he'd slept on the bed with me. I had also grown accustomed to sleeping in ambient light ever since removing the blackout curtains that used to make the room into a tomb. The sleep mask helped.

It was still dark outside and would be for another hour and a half or so. I found that if I fell asleep while it was still dark, it was much easier to stay asleep when the sun began to rise. I flipped off the light switch, crawled into bed, and slipped into dreamland.

• • •

A blinding white light and the sound of Charlie barking like a rabid dog on fire woke me from an otherwise dead sleep. If not for the horrifying alarm of my mad dog, I would have assumed the sun had simply risen. It was not the sun.

I felt the familiar hum of the UFO before I heard it, and was frozen to the bed in immediate fear. Charlie kept barking and snarled in between breaths.

When the humming sound and vibration grew more intense, Charlie stopped barking suddenly, whimpered once, and ran through the open bedroom door. I heard his nails click all the way down the stairs into the living room. He'd abandoned me and I couldn't blame him. Nothing ever made my dog turn into a coward. I wasn't ready for this.

An unseen weight pushed down on my chest and the breath was forced out of my lungs. My heart beat fast and a thin sheen of sweat covered my body. Because of the heat, I only wore my boxers and they were already damp with perspiration. I knew I should do something, try to move, but I was riveted to the spot. I tried to force my mind to move an arm or a leg, unable to tell if I was paralyzed by fear or something else.

The hum grew louder, and the light became so bright that no shadows could hide in its wake. I wish I could tell you that I was infinitely brave in that moment and held onto my urine, refusing to pee on myself, but to do so would be dishonest and diminish the level of fear that overwhelmed me.

An instant later the all-consuming light blinked out. I was blinded by the darkness and purplish ghost spots that dotted my vision. The terrible thing I had been obsessing over for months had arrived. My personal terror was near its apex. There was no time to assess the danger and fight. The situation was out of my control. Despite my will and desire to avoid it, I was forced into facing the worst experience of my life.

As soon as my eyes adjusted to the gloom and I made out the shape of the bedroom door, I jerked my body free from its frozen state and made a run for the hallway. I'd only gone about two and a half strides toward freedom when the hum and the bright light returned with a vengeance. Newly blind from the sudden reversal I stumbled and fell to the floor. My surprised cry caused Charlie to bark from his safe location downstairs. As I tried to push myself up, the muscles in my arms stiffened and I was pulled across the floor by an invisible force. My scream was stifled in the back of my throat.

Out of my periphery, I saw a creature similar to the one I'd seen on that lonely country road. It might have even been the same one. The main difference between this one and the other was that this one seemed to be smiling with its lipless mouth, where the other one communicated no emotion with its face and spoke only with its hateful, penetrating eyes. I tried to scream again in vain. Black spots invaded my vision. I was going to pass out.

I tried hard to control my breathing in order to get enough oxygen to my brain. I needed to be conscious in case there was any chance of escape. The monstrous dwarf-like creature walked across the room and opened a bedroom window. A beam of elastic light brighter than the already blinding light twisted into the room. It was a sort of flexible laser beam tentacle that I had never seen before or since. The creature that invited this anomaly into my room reached out and touched the beam of light, then disappeared in a flash.

My heart started pounding again and I knew I was going to lose consciousness. My vision blurred, but I stayed focused as the beam reached out into the room. It swept back and forth as if it was blind. It was a good thing I was an easy target since I was unable to move. It came closer and I felt the tentacle's white-hot heat touch the skin of my forearm and I was, for lack of a better explanation, transported somewhere else in an instant.

Dark gunmetal walls lined both sides of an oval chamber. I lay on the ground, restrained by the same invisible force that kept me paralyzed in bed. My boxer shorts were gone and I was completely naked. At least they'd had the decency to flip me face up. Many expressionless grey faces with black eyes filled with ancient knowledge moved in and out of my line of sight. I had no idea how many there were. It was impossible to keep track of them all.

I felt something like fingers coated in slime poke and prod my prone body. That was followed by a sensation like needles being pushed into various parts of my body, causing my nerves to lash out in pain. I was a sort of reverse acupuncture, designed to inflict the maximum amount of pain instead of relieving it. My throat and vocal cords were stuck in suspended animation, just like the rest of my body. My tear ducts still worked, however, and hot liquid spilled down the side of my head into my ears. I regretted my decision to remain awake and wished I had been turned face down and knocked unconscious to be blissfully ignorant of the torment I endured, but I had no such luck.

The most horrifying and difficult to describe experience came next. I'm still not sure exactly what happened, but I was somehow forced into copulation with one of the aliens. I have no idea if it was male or female, or remember if I was ever physically touched. What I do remember was that I felt nothing except the excruciating pain of my nerve endings exploding from the needle torture, and in the next instant my pain was doubled and combined with the sensation of the most powerful orgasm I'd ever had. It was the most intense pain coupled with the most intense pleasure. I assume the combination of unbearable pain and explosive pleasure is what most of the people into S & M and bondage would consider the height of exhilaration, but not me. I felt dirty, used up, and humiliated. I am not ashamed to say that a flood of tears poured from my eyes.

As my body reacted to what I felt was the height of its endurance, I blacked out. My senses were finally overloaded and my mind could no longer withstand the abuse I suffered. In the blackness there was a measure of peace. I wished for death, if only to never go through that kind of hell again.

I regained consciousness sometime later. I was laid out on the same cold stone floor, still unable to move. More grey faces and soulless black eyes approached me. If the creatures talked I never heard them. The only sound was the constant low-frequency hum of the ship we rode in. I closed my eyes for just a second, hoping for some relief, then reopened them. As much as I wanted to blot out the memory of this experience, I needed to be aware of whatever was thrown at me.

Cold, moist hands moved me into a kneeling position. One of the grey beasts approached me. It was slightly taller standing as I was on my knees at its full height. I was forced to look into its eyes. Staring into those inky pools of blackness was like staring into the essence of non-existence. My spirit was obliterated by their depth, and I was terrified of the consequences of being lost in the vastness that existed behind them.

The forced examination of my soul was worse than any physical torture. I felt the sensation of its mind digging into the folds of my brain. Nothing was hidden from it; not my outward actions or my most private thoughts. All of me was evaluated with a clinical coldness that measured my value by how much could be used against me. Don't ask how I knew this. Perhaps my brain picked up on some of the thoughts the creature projected onto me. I don't know for sure.

The mental intrusion lasted far longer than was comfortable for me, but I was less afraid than before. My fear was replaced by anger at having been violated in every way imaginable. And the little grey beast picked up the emotions I felt in that moment and probed deeper into my mind. I wondered later if it had trouble understanding the free will nature of my being. I became convinced that I was correct about that intuition.

After the invasion into my thoughts, I was left in complete darkness, alone and unrestrained. I had no idea if I was in the same oval room as before or moved to a new location. By that point, I was so exhausted that I laid down on the hard floor and fell asleep. I was grateful for the opportunity to be unconscious and unaware of my surroundings. I had no dreams.

• • •

Sometime later, a beam of light like the one that preceded my trip to that cold, dark place, woke me from my nap. I was able to see the full shape of the room. It was an oval, similar to the chamber I arrived in and had the same dull metal color and texture. The sides were smooth, about fifteen feet high, and impossible to climb. I wondered if the holding cell was similar to purgatory; a waiting room between worlds. What I thought about the chain of events during my abduction didn't really matter too much to my captors. I braced myself for what came next.

My body was paralyzed once more. Drool spilled out of the side of my mouth as I floated toward the light. A violent tremor wracked my body. I'd never had a seizure before, but every muscle in my body clenched, forced into a state of rigor mortis. This was different somehow from my earlier paralysis, as though this specific action was intended to torment me even further.

As I moved closer to the top edge of the room, little grey bodies with huge black eyes peered over the edge, examining me with their inscrutable stares, enjoying the fear emanating from my every pore.

After my body crested the opening, I floated down a dark hallway and passed over what looked like the inside of a hatch. There was a distinct circle cut into the metal below me. Curved cracks appeared on its surface. There was a mechanical whooshing sound as the barrier disappeared. Even with my head frozen in place, I could tell that it was an opening to the earth below. The limited view of the canopy of trees far below was breathtaking and terrifying at the same time. I floated above the opening and there was nothing to stop me from falling to my death other than the invisible force keeping me in the air.

I breathed faster and my pulse sped up. I felt myself slip through the portal and hyperventilated as the sensation of a free fall washed over me. Wind whipped around me like a violent gale, and I plummeted toward certain death. I considered what might come after death. I was never the religious type and considered most religions to be man-made inventions used to control the behavior of the masses. There was no time to reconsider the possibility that I was wrong about my worldview as darkness consumed me and I blacked out.

• 11 •

I woke up gasping for breath, disoriented. As soon as I recognized my bedroom I screamed as loud as I could. My cries were no longer stifled. I paused long enough to catch a breath, then continued screaming. Charlie appeared at the threshold of the bedroom and barked like he did when a stranger knocked on the front door. I was no stranger, but the unbridled screaming scared him. I took another hitching breath, tried to rein in the madness taking over me, fell back onto my sweat-soaked pillow and cried.

I had no idea what time it was, and it took several minutes to come down from the shock of being suddenly awake after assuming I was dead. Charlie kept his distance. He'd stopped barking but refused to enter the room. His head was lowered and his hackles were up as he snarled in my general direction. I lacked the energy to engage him. His disorientation at my sudden mysterious return was the least of my problems.

In a first attempt to get out of bed, I leaned on an

elbow and collapsed onto my side. I couldn't move. It wasn't like before when I was paralyzed against my will. My body was exhausted from the punishment it had been subjected to and refused to cooperate with my efforts to get out of bed. My will to fight was depleted. I stopped trying to roll out of bed and slipped into a deep sleep.

I dreamed of the monstrous things that had been done to me. Any other nightmare I'd ever had in my life paled in comparison to that one. I moaned and thrashed as I relived the abduction and torture through the lens of the surreal world only dreams can create.

When I woke up sometime later it was dark. I had no idea if it was the same day, the next, or another day of the week. I ached from everywhere that was possible to ache. People like to say they feel like they have been hit by a truck when they have been in an accident or are suffering from a bad cold. I felt like I had been flattened in an industrial laundry press and run back through several times for good measure.

When I moved my arm in an attempt to roll myself out of bed the muscles screamed out in excruciating pain. I was nearly blinded by the pain but forced myself to continue. I needed to go to the bathroom and refused to pee on myself again.

I worked myself into a sitting position on the side of the bed with my feet on the floor. Before I could think too much, I pushed myself up to stand and paid dearly for my effort. The pain exploded from my feet through my body into the nerves in my eyelids, setting off alarms in my head. If I possessed a lesser level of pride I would have urinated all over myself right there and collapsed into bed, but my body would not allow it.

Each step I took toward the bathroom was devastating. Every movement brought a crashing wave of pain. My legs were like dead weight as I stumbled toward the hallway. I leaned against the doorjamb and rested. Charlie lay on the floor and looked up at me. I took several deep breaths and contemplated stopping and peeing right there.

I passed through the door and used the wall in the hallway for support as I inched my way forward. I entered the bathroom and shuffled over to the toilet in the dark. I was glad I only had to pee because anything else would have sapped the last of my energy. I didn't bother flushing when I was done and only washed my hands out of pure stubbornness. Even the lukewarm water and aloe infused hand soap felt like razors cutting into my skin with an added splash of lemon juice for good measure.

As I shuffled my way back into the bedroom, Charlie lifted his head to look at me. He wasn't barking anymore but was still wary of my presence. I wondered if there was some scent or essence that was passed onto me by my tormentors. I leaned against the door for a moment and regarded him with sadness.

I struggled to stay upright as I ambled toward my bed and fell into it. As I plunged back into unconsciousness, Charlie trotted into the room and launched himself onto the bed. He wedged his back against mine and gave a single huff before settling into position. I felt the warmth of his body and shuddered against the sudden chill I felt in the room.

● ● ●

It was still dark when I opened my eyes again. I still felt pain and stiffness in my joints, but it was a stitch more bearable than it was before. I was still exhausted but could manage a thought without being consumed by the pain. I lifted my head to peer into the darkness. Charlie shifted beside me but did not rise from sleep.

I jumped at the sound of my phone vibrating on the nightstand near my head. I always placed it facedown to block out the light. It vibrated again and the light of the display leaked out from under it. I grabbed the phone too late and missed the incoming call. The clock told me it was just past four in the morning. The display still showed the missed call. It was work. I had no energy to deal with my boss Lonnie. I set the phone down. I'd have to call him back later.

I became aware at some point that I was covered in a sheen of sweat. My boxers were soaked and a sour smell emanated from my body; the kind of smell a person gets when they fail to clean themselves at all after a week of hard labor or sickness. The chills I had earlier passed and my temperature felt more or less normal. Any fever I might have had that caused the night sweats dissipated the moment I rose out of the depths of my dream world.

I picked up my phone and did a double take as I checked the date. It was Saturday. The last thing I remembered it was Wednesday evening. I was supposed to be back to work late afternoon on Thursday. I'd somehow missed two days of work. And I didn't call in. I knew that I was in trouble, if not out of a job.

I was tempted to set my phone back down and pretend I didn't see the date. I closed my eyes and sighed. Always a glutton for punishment, my mindless sense of loyalty and responsibility prevented me from blowing off work and falling back to sleep. Over the years I'd been able to sock away a bit of money, but I still needed my job.

There were a total of four messages on my voicemail. The first and third were from my boss, who I hardly ever saw. I don't know what I was expecting, but he seemed genuinely concerned about me. It was so out of character for me to miss a day for any reason, and to not call was practically announcing my death. I was surprised no one had come to the house with how worried he sounded.

The other two were from my coworker and occasional confidant, Alicia. She was worried about me. The thought of relaying my most recent experience to her made my stomach churn. A wave of anxiety spread out from my chest and I was unable to even consider moving from the bed. Charlie whined in his sleep. I wondered if my strange behavior was rubbing off on him.

In no condition to call my boss, I set the phone down and lay back down on the bed. My heart started to race as I allowed myself to recall the things that had happened to me. Two and a half days had passed without my knowledge or permission. It was like I'd lost a weekend partying, but with none of the fun.

I rolled over onto my stomach and inched my way backwards to the edge of the bed. I had to stand and begin the process of getting on with life. I lost my footing, slid onto the floor and sunk to my knees on the rug. I found myself in a praying position but was in no mood to seek spiritual counsel. I put my hands on the edge of the bed and pushed myself up. My legs were wobbly and I felt unbalanced, but I managed to stand.

I took tentative steps in the dark toward the door, refusing to reach for the light switch in case turning the lights on revealed something I did not want to see. I had no particular destination in mind but thought some soap and water might not be a bad idea. By the time I reached the bedroom door, I had the urge to use the bathroom again. With some effort, I made it to the toilet in the dark and sank onto the hard plastic seat. I closed my eyes. What I couldn't see wouldn't hurt me.

I must have dozed off at some point since it was no longer pitch dark when I opened my eyes again. Weak light filtered into the room from the little window in the bathtub. I stood up with some effort and walked into the hallway which had turned a dark grey. The sun was rising in the east and would continue to push away the shadows of the night until the light displaced the dark.

I took a step toward the stairs and looked down. My view of the space beyond was limited. It seemed like an awful long way to go, but if I was to get on with life I had to do make the trek sometime. I grabbed the banister and used it to guide myself down the steps. Progress was slow as I took one excruciating step at a time. By the time I reached the bottom, the ambient light in the house had brightened to a light grey. A shiver passed through me as I remembered the outer skin of the aliens. I decided I didn't like that color and never would.

I used the wall for support and hobbled into the kitchen. I stopped in front of the coffee maker. I wanted a cup of coffee in a bad way. It took considerable effort to find the can, put a few scoops in the filter, and dump some fresh water into the reservoir. By the time I pressed the button to start the brewing process, I was spent. I shuffled to a kitchen chair, slumped into it, and laid my head on the hard surface of the table.

When I next opened my eyes the mid-morning sun blazed through the blinds and curtains. There were no more shades of grey. I closed my eyes and moaned.

The light was too bright and I felt exposed. It didn't help that aside from my soiled boxers I was naked. I wanted to hide underneath a dark blanket or crawl into a hole somewhere. I raised my head and caught sight of my sunglasses on top of a pile of junk mail. I slipped them on, closed my eyes, and sighed.

With an unreasonable amount of effort, I stood and ambled my way back to the kitchen. I grabbed a coffee cup off the counter and sloshed some of the coffee into it. I lacked the energy to add cream and sugar. It tasted bitter with a slight burnt taste that shocked some of my senses back to life. As another rush of the swill ran down my throat the thought of Carla's perfect coffee taunted me.

A knock on the door caused me to drop the cup. It hit the side of the counter and crashed to the tile floor. The cup exploded in a spectacular display as hot coffee splashed against my legs. I moaned in surprise but hardly felt the hot liquid burn my skin. Charlie bolted down the stairs, barking like crazy. He rushed past the kitchen toward the front door.

I leaned over to pick up the larger pieces of the broken cup and the knock on the door came again, louder and more insistent. I came up too fast and banged my head on the bottom of an open cupboard door. The impact made my already unsteady world swoon. I cried out in pain and threw out a few unsavory words. Charlie kept right on barking and I lacked the energy to make him stop.

As the sharpness of the initial pain of the cupboard door digging into my head passed, I stood to my full height, held the top of my head, and crossed the living room to the front door. I heard Alicia's muffled voice as she knocked again. Charlie circled in front of the door, anxious to see who was waiting on the porch.

"Alex, open up. It's Alicia."

I swung open the front door and Alicia took a step back, perhaps shocked by my appearance. I wondered what I looked like since I hadn't dared to look in the bathroom mirror, but it must have been pretty bad. Charlie bounded toward her, but ever the gentleman tried to control his excitement. He wagged his tail and she patted him on the head. Embarrassed, I remembered I was dressed in nothing more than my underwear and a pair of sunglasses.

Alicia confirmed my suspicions about my appearance. "My God Alex. You look terrible."

"Thanks." I rocked back and forth on my heels and felt warm blood where I'd banged my head.

She gave me a concerned look. "Can I come in?"

I motioned her inside and shut the door, leaving my dog outside. It had probably been days since he'd been out in the yard. I felt a twinge of guilt for neglecting him.

Alicia stood in the entryway and scanned the living room and dining room beyond before turning her attention back to me. "Is everything okay, Alex? You haven't been to work in two days and everyone is worried about you. And you look and smell awful."

I was irritated at her last jab, but she seemed to take a genuine interest in my well being. Unable to confess the awful truth, I lied. "I've been sick, but am feeling a little better today. I think maybe I had a touch of the flu or something."

Alicia grew serious. "Well, you better give Lonnie a call. He was getting ready to give you the boot for the no call, no show two days in a row. I told him I'd come check on you to make sure you were still alive."

Feeling my detachment from reality increase, I turned to her and said with little inflection, "I'll give him a call right after you leave. I promise."

"You better. We need you back at work. You're the reliable one, and John can be quite unbearable as I'm sure you know."

"Oh, I know," I said and forced a smile as I swayed back and forth like a drunk.

Alicia persisted to press me for answers. "Are you sure you're feeling alright, aside from the flu I mean? You seem different somehow."

Different how, I wondered, but didn't say out loud. "It must be because I'm so exhausted. This bug has really kicked my butt."

She appeared to accept that answer, but I could tell there was a bit of skepticism in her tone. "Well, make sure to take care of yourself, Alex. I'm just glad to know you are still alive, and I hope you feel better soon. Please call me if you need anything. And give Lonnie a call, too."

"Thanks, Alicia. I will. Sorry for causing so much trouble for everyone. Time just seemed to have slipped away from me."

I opened the door to let her out, hoping that she would just leave without another word. If she kept pushing I was likely to tell her everything, and I really couldn't deal with all the concern and sympathy she seemed ready to pour out on me.

Alicia stopped and turned back before walking off the porch. "I'm serious, Alex. If you need anything, call me anytime, day or night."

Her concern touched me. There was not another person who'd come to visit me in years. On the verge of tears, I thanked her again and watched her get into her car and pull out of the driveway. She honked as she turned onto the main road. Charlie bounded across the porch from the yard and into the house, as I closed the door behind the two of us. I had quite a mess to clean up in the kitchen.

• 12 •

Shortly after Alicia left, I called my boss Lonnie and tried to explain my absence. I made up a partial lie about having a fever that made me delirious and that I'd lost track of time. He was less understanding than Alicia but was glad to hear I was still alive. I knew there was no way I'd face any discipline over the situation. I was a model employee who was known for my extreme reliability. If he knew half of the things my coworkers did that I covered for, my couple of days out with no contact would seem like nothing.

I walked back upstairs in slow motion toward the bathroom to see why Alicia had such a strong reaction to my appearance. I stood before the mirror in the dim light that filtered through the small window behind the shower curtain. I knew I must have looked awful. I already knew my smell was enough to knock a person over. Something about the haunted look on Alicia's face when she saw me gave me an idea that it was worse than I envisioned.

I closed my eyes before flipping the light switch

and braced myself. It took a few seconds to adjust to the bright vanity lights above the medicine cabinet mirror. I opened my eyes cautiously and nearly jumped away from my own reflection when I caught sight of myself. It was as bad as I expected and worse. My hair was pointed in all directions with one side smashed down flat and it looked like someone had dumped a bucket of grease over my head. I looked exhausted and there were dark purple circles that looked like bruises under both of my eyes. The skin on my face looked sallow and waxy. My cheeks were sunken in.

I turned away, shut off the light, and sat down on the toilet. I put my face in my hands and sobbed. My stifled emotions caught up with me and the tears flowed. Any numbness I felt was replaced with raw emotion. I hitched as I let out all the pent-up grief until all I could hear was my own blubbering. I wanted to be brave and shove it all down, but courage was a mask I could not wear that day.

When the crying subsided, I leaned over and turned on the hot water to draw a bath. While the water filled the tub, I closed my eyes and put my head in my hands. The sound of the running stream was comforting, and I craved the thought of slipping into the near scalding water. Without thinking, I slipped out of my boxers and stepped into the tub. It was almost too hot, but that didn't stop me from lowering myself into it. I rested my head against the back wall and allowed the warmth to work its way into my muscles and bones. I closed my eyes and sighed.

My euphoria was short lived. Behind my eyelids, I saw the face of one of those little grey beasts. Its thin lips formed a wicked toothless smile and those too big eyes pierced my soul with their condemnation and guilt. My body jerked involuntarily, and my eyes flew open. Water splashed around me. My beating heart pushed adrenaline through my veins and I felt ready to act on my primal fight or flight instincts.

With my eyes open, I took a deep breath and forced my rigid body to relax. The grey monster behind my eyes was not real. I knew deep down I was telling myself a lie and I needed that lie to gain control of my faculties.

Unwilling to admit the full truth I created and repeated a simple mantra. "I am home. I am safe."

"Home. Safe."

"Home. Safe."

While I said those words, another little voice inside contradicted my self-deception. After all, it was from my home that I was snatched out of and tortured like some rat in a lab experiment gone wrong. My home was my zone of comfort and safety, and that had been violated. Now nowhere was safe. Nothing was sacred.

I had hoped that the hot bath would have relaxed my body and mind, but it had the opposite effect. I felt more paranoid than ever. I slid deeper into the tub, hoping that forcing myself to stay in the hot water would somehow trick my mind into believing my lies. It didn't work very well. I refused to close my eyes again for fear I would see one of those little monsters.

I had to see Carla. She'd know what to do.

Something else that didn't strike me until that moment was that I hadn't seen Charlie in a while. He'd been around me but had not directly engaged me. Being used to the bachelor life I never closed the bathroom door and my faithful companion was almost always by my side. I turned my head toward the open door and strained to see past the threshold. The house was too quiet. Where was my dog?

I pushed myself up in the tub, a new dread dripping into my veins like a demonic IV. I refused to let my thoughts wander to worrying about my only friend. I whistled loudly and called for him. "Charlie. Come here, boy."

There was no response.

I tried again with a notable tremble in my voice. "Charlie. Come here, boy."

Again there was nothing.

I sank back into the tub, wishing for a way to be washed down the drain and escape my problems forever. The clacking of dog nails against the hardwood floor brought a rush of relief over me. But all was not well. The click-clack of his pace was slow and deliberate, as if Charlie was approaching me with caution. The IV drip of fear returned. I craned my head as far as I could from the tub in an attempt to catch a glimpse of my beloved companion.

His head crested the stairs first, and he regarded me as though I were a dangerous stranger. He refused to growl at me, but his ears were laid back flat against his head. When his body was visible, I could see his tail was tucked underneath his body. He assumed a self-protective posture and moved toward me slowly. My heart could have broken. Charlie had never acted that way toward me before. But even he knew something was different about me.

Making no sudden movements that might scare him off, I took my arm out of the tub with my palm turned up, allowing the water to drip onto the floor. I looked to the corner of the bathroom to not make direct eye contact with my dog. I had to appear submissive if I wanted him to come near me.

His cautiousness never wavered as he plodded forward. In a soft voice, I spoke to him. "Come here, Charlie. Good boy. Daddy missed you, my good boy."

He seemed to take the bait as he came closer. A fleeting thought of my dog chomping down on my hand and tearing it to shreds crossed my mind. I tried hard to ignore it. If I showed fear now, I'd lose him.

When he was within a foot of my dripping hand, I turned my head to face him. His ears relaxed a bit and his tail came out from between his legs. He took another step forward and started to lick the water off my hand. It tickled so badly that I wanted to pull my hand away, but I didn't dare. The moment was too fragile.

After a few seconds, I gave him a scratch under the chin. His ears went back to their neutral position and he allowed me to pet him on the top of his head. His tail started wagging and it seemed like he was returning to normal. I pet him for a good while until he had his fill of me, turned and trotted away, the click-clack of his nails following him as he went.

I sat in the tub for another fifteen minutes or so, contemplating my next move. I needed to see Carla right away. It was Saturday and the Avondale Paranormal Society met that night. My dark thoughts lifted considerably at the idea of sharing my experience with her. And with any luck, Phil and Ellie Durst would be there too. And maybe others.

• 13 •

I had intended to be at Carla's house early to get a few minutes alone with her and talk about my experience before the meeting started. An accident on the main road from my house to Avondale thwarted those plans. I ended up at her house ten minutes after the meeting was scheduled to start. I sat in my truck outside her house and looked at the door. The warm light coming from the front picture window was inviting. I thought about pulling away and going back home.

Instead of indulging my cowardice, I got out of the truck and walked toward the house. The closer I came to the front door the stronger the sweet smell of coffee and fresh baked chocolate chip cookies became. Inhaling the sugary scent had an instant calming effect on my nerves. It was the right thing coming here. I reached out and rang the bell.

Carla greeted me a moment later. She was still in her apron from baking. Her hair and eyes were as wild as ever. She gave me a big, sweet smile and motioned for me to come in. "Come on in, stranger. We haven't even started yet."

As she walked me into the living room, she motioned to the couple sitting on the sofa to the right. "You remember Phil and Ellie Durst, don't you, Alex?"

A lump in my throat prevented me from answering right away. That lump was a direct result of the fact that I was seeing an entirely different couple from the one I had seen at that first meeting. After a second look, I realized it was them, but they had changed somehow. They looked younger. More like fresh-faced hipsters than the aging couple I had met before, who were trying desperately to hold onto the vestiges of youth that had long passed them by.

"Yes, I remember them," I stammered, trying not to be awkward.

Phil stood up and put his hand out. I took it and shook his hand. It felt strange touching flesh that appeared to be younger than my own, but I knew was not. What I saw and felt could not be possible, yet there it was. The couple I was gawking at was at least thirty years younger than the people I had seen before. I had the sudden urge to leave when Ellie gave me a big smile with a subtle reptilian quality that made my skin crawl.

In a charming voice, Ellie cooed, "Oh, Alex it's so good to see you. We just never seemed to cross paths. I am so glad you could make it to the meeting tonight. Carla tells me you have some news to share."

I whipped my head toward Carla, who looked unaffected. I had not told her anything about my abduction and subsequent torture.

Carla spoke. "Ellie, it really has been too long. That thing with Alex happened nearly two months ago now, you silly goose."

Ellie blushed and held up her arms in a *who me?* gesture that struck me as insincere. And it is also entirely possible that I imagined her insincerity, but I could have sworn that I saw Carla's eyes, normally so warm and inviting even if a little wild, glint toward Ellie with something that looked like malice. My paranoia was getting the best of me. I took a seat in one of the mismatched chairs.

Carla brought over a tray with coffee, tea, and her famous chocolate chip cookies. I poured myself a cup of coffee and added too much cream and sugar. I also took two of the cookies and sunk into the back of the armchair. It was the most secure I'd felt in days.

The meeting started with Carla updating the group on her latest research into the reason for abductions and sightings. None of her information was particularly insightful or new and consisted of a reiteration of the most plausible theories for alien interest in humans from a distinctly human perspective. I'd like to repeat it, but it went in one ear and out the other.

Carla then started a round robin, asking the group to share anything that was on our minds. Phil and Ellie went first. I don't remember much of what they said either as I was focused on what I would say. My mouth felt dry. I took a sip of coffee and bit off a chunk of soft, warm cookie. The taste combination should have been steps away from heaven, but the coffee tasted bitter and the cookie too sweet. My stomach churned.

Ellie said something that I didn't hear at all. She stopped talking, looked at me, and touched my arm. A strange electric feeling similar to static shock passed through me and I jerked away from her, nearly sloshing hot coffee all over my shirt.

"Sorry Alex. I didn't mean to startle you." She

looked sincerely concerned for me.

I felt like an idiot and wondered what was wrong with me. "No, no. Please don't apologize. I'm just a little jumpy."

I set the coffee cup down and struggled to find a way to verbalize my abduction and torture to this small group of people that were the closest thing I had to friends in those days. I ignored the sinking feeling in my lower bowels, warning me not to say anything out loud. My brain argued that if I didn't get it out, if I didn't tell someone, it would destroy me.

I burst into hot, embarrassed tears as I told the story. I thought I'd moved past the emotion somehow in the past couple of days, as though it was easy to forget how violated and helpless I'd been. But all I had done in between short periods of grief was build up a wall of denial and avoid thinking about it. It's something I'd always done as a way of protecting myself from trauma.

As I sat there and sobbed, Carla came over and put her hand on my back. Ellie reached her hand out again to touch my arm. There was no electric spark that time, just the warmth of her hand. All of their empathy and attempts to provide comfort made me cry harder. I stopped trying to hold back and wept until I could not go on any longer. After I overcame my initial sense of shame at crying in front of other people, it felt good to release everything I tried so hard to push down inside.

When my tears stopped, I sat in silence while Carla wrapped up the meeting. I blocked out most of what she said, but there was something that caught my attention.

"Well, I attended the conference in Lake Jarvis, and that went pretty well. Of course, I ran into Ron Lincoln and we got into a pretty heated debate before I just had to walk away. I can't stand him and his crackpot theories."

"Who's Ron Lincoln? " I said so low it was possible the question went unnoticed.

Carla paused. "What did you say, Alex?"

A bit more alert and able to assert myself I asked again, "Who is Ron Lincoln? I've never heard that name before."

Carla visibly stiffened, a clear signal of her revulsion at having to talk about the man. "Ron is someone you don't need to bother yourself with. He is a pest and just trying to stir up trouble."

She was evading the question so I pushed harder. "I get that you don't like him, but what is it that he does or says that is so troublesome to you?"

"Alex, really. You don't trust me by now. Ron is stuck on a theory about aliens that I cannot even bear to repeat. Needless to say, it has roots in religious superstition and the belief that humans are the only intelligent life form in all of space. Can you imagine? How ridiculous?"

She threw her hands up in the air and laughed. Ellie covered a smirk and Phil chuckled right along with them. I stared at Phil and Ellie, studying them. Their skin was supple and young, but in their eyes was a depth of experience that comes with age. Something was not right with those two. Instead of confronting the issue, I avoided it and hoped not to draw attention to the fact that I knew how strange it was that they looked three decades younger than the first time I met them.

"Yeah, that does sound crazy." I sat back in my chair, tired of trying to think of a way to get the whole story of Ron Lincoln out of Carla. I was learning that it was typical of her to sidestep a direct line of questioning if it didn't fit in with her ideology. But something about what she said resonated with me. After all, the only perspective concerning the subject of aliens that I'd been consistently exposed to was Carla's. And when I challenged her, she was quick to dismiss the things I pointed out. I made a mental note of the name, Ron Lincoln, and filed it away to look into later.

● ● ●

While at home later that evening, I tried searching for Ron Lincoln and his pet theology on the internet. He didn't have a website or even a blog of his own, but there were plenty of people with criticisms of his arguments. What was most interesting was that none of the people refuting his claims were able to articulate his side of the argument. Most of what I found online were personal insults and jabs at the man's character. A few set out to prove how insane it was that he refuted arguments for evolution and the validity of the possibility of life on other planets. The one thing I could not find was what, if anything, he believed the UFOs and aliens to be.

It was entirely possible that he denied the existence of them altogether, but how could anyone deny the shared similarity of so many experiences over so many years. It seemed to defy logic to simply disregard the sheer number of people that claimed to have seen UFO's, or been abducted by aliens. He must have another theory, but what was it?

In one of my searches, I ran across an ad for a

presentation taking place during the UFO festival in Roswell, New Mexico; the city made famous for the 1947 UFO crash. I discovered that the madman was some sort of doctor, as the ad referred to him as Dr. Ron Lincoln. He was scheduled to make an appearance and give a talk on the second day of the two-day alien celebration titled, *What are these aliens among us?* That struck me as odd considering the majority of those who believed in aliens thought they were beings from other planets. If they were not creatures from out space, what were they?

I walked away from my laptop and tried to concentrate on something else, anything else. I took Charlie for a walk, watched TV, and even tried reading a book. None of that could deter me from the idea that information about Dr. Lincoln and his theories were being purposely withheld from me by Carla and his online dissenters. If I wanted to find out what the man believed, I'd have to find some way to reach out to him personally.

• 14 •

The first night back at work was the worst. Of course, when I arrived it was still late afternoon with the hot sun blazing down on the pavement and weeds around the factory. I sat in the guard shack and watched the sun slip further and further into the western sky, wondering what I would do when it disappeared altogether.

It was well past six when the last car left the parking lot. I waved at the driver, and couldn't help thinking that the sound of the clanging gate was a signal of my impending doom. The chain moved slowly along the track, trapping me inside the confines of the perimeter fence. My stomach fluttered as my mind conjured up the image of the cold dark room in the alien craft I was transferred to before being transported back to my own bed.

In an attempt to stop myself from thinking about being locked in, and dreading the setting sun, I tried to think of new ways to contact Dr. Lincoln. He had no phone number, email, or social media accounts that could be found by searching the internet. By all measures, the man seemed invisible. There were many people who discussed and debunked his theories, but my attempts at direct contact were met with a dead end.

As I made the first perimeter check after darkness swallowed up the light, I considered the possibility of taking a trip to Roswell to see Dr. Lincoln in person. I could grab a ticket to his presentation and take some of my accumulated vacation time to explore the U.S. city best known for UFO and alien activity. A trip to the desert might be just what I needed to shake me out of my surroundings and help me forget about my troubles. I might even find some answers there.

As I continued walking, lost in my own head, the light of the guard shack came into view. I managed to make it around the factory without falling apart. It was a small victory and I allowed myself a little smile. Granted, I simply avoided thinking about what might be lurking in the dark while I circled the building, but it was better than confronting the fear head on and becoming a blubbering mess. It made the following rounds that night much easier.

Alicia arrived early, much to my surprise. I told her about my potential travel plans and her face lit up.

"I've always wanted to visit Roswell. It would be so fun to go to all the cheesy little shops and tourist traps." Her smile was infectious. "I could even see if I can find some things for you to do while you're out there."

It was clear that she wanted to help and I lacked the energy to argue.

"Go ahead and plan the trip, but remember I'm on a budget. I'm not sure I'll be visiting any corny sideshow attractions, but give me the information anyway."

She beamed at the prospect of planning my trip. "I'm so excited for you, Alex. I'll make sure it's fun, and that you get to see this Dr. Ron Lincoln. And I'll try not to overdo the cheese factor."

I smiled and thanked her. I considered telling her about my close encounter of the fourth kind and the real reason for my trip, but I just couldn't. Although I had already spilled the details of my experience with Carla, Phil, and Ellie; this was different. I thought of Alicia as more than just a coworker or a distant acquaintance. She was a friend, and opening myself up to her required a level of vulnerability that I was not ready to expose.

I stuck around after the scheduled end of my shift and waited with Alicia for John to show up. He was late as usual and greeted me with his typical side smirk, like we had some inside joke only he understood. "I sure am glad to see you, Alex. I was beginning to worry that we might lose you."

If I wasn't looking right at him I would have rolled my eyes. His only true concern was that he didn't have to cover part of my shift for me, and that he no longer had to be worried about showing up for work on time. I thanked him as briefly as I could and stepped out of the guard shack.

Alicia walked out behind me. I turned around and it was clear she had a question to ask me.

"Alex, what happened to you? I don't know how I know, let's call it women's intuition, but you had something more than just a little sickness, didn't you?"

I struggled to find the right words. It was harder to talk to her then it was talking to Carla and the rest of the Avondale Paranormal Society. I think that was because I was able to shut them out of my real life. Again

I had the desire to tell her the whole story, but fear prevented me from letting her get too close.

"I...You're right that it was more than just a touch of the flu. It's a pretty long story, though. Maybe I can fill you in later?"

Alicia's eyes lit up again. "Okay. We'll talk later. Have a good rest of the night Alex."

"You too." My stomach was in knots as I contemplated sharing my experience with her.

● ● ●

The ride home that night was stressful. I sped as fast as I dared down the dark, wooded two-lane road. My eyes stayed focused on the blacktop ahead of me. It was dangerous to drive that way, but I couldn't risk seeing anything lurking on the dirt shoulder that had no business being there. I'd driven these roads countless times and the landscape was familiar, but I felt like a stranger in the place I'd lived my entire life.

I pulled into the driveway and sat in the truck for a few moments. My whole body was trembling and I hadn't realized how fast my heart was beating until that moment. I looked at the garage and connecting breezeway. It was mostly unlit and I decided I'd stay parked in the driveway. There were shadows in there I didn't like with too many places for things to hide.

My hands felt clammy as I contemplated getting out of the truck. I swallowed my growing anxiety and opened the door fast. I stood outside for a moment, breathing in the warm night air. Frogs and crickets played their night time songs and an owl hooted somewhere in the distance. The porch light shone like a beacon.

I forced myself to walk toward the front steps and trotted to the door. I fumbled with my keys. The shaking in my hands prevented me from sticking the house key into the hole on the first try. When I did unlock and open the door, Charlie bounded out and greeted with me a wagging tail, wet kisses on the palm of my hand, and the excitement of a puppy. I patted him on the head and stepped inside.

I breathed a sigh of relief as I shut the door behind me. Charlie circled me, demanding my attention. I knelt down and scrubbed his ears. His hind leg started thumping out an unintelligible beat. I laughed and scrubbed harder. Just as it seemed there was no more he could take, I stopped and pet him with a gentle stroke. Satisfied, he padded away from me into some far corner of the house.

I thought about my upcoming vacation. My primary goal of meeting Dr. Lincoln trumped any ideas of relaxing or having fun. He was only scheduled for one session, but I was determined to take full advantage of his time. I allowed myself to hope that he had some answers to the questions Carla avoided.

I sat down at the kitchen table and opened my laptop to research flights, car rentals, rooms, and tickets to the UFO Festival. I'd forgotten that I agreed to let Alicia plan my trip until I checked my email. In the time it took me to drive home, she'd found a red-eye flight on an economy airline, a gas sipping car rental, and an inexpensive hotel a short distance from the conference center. She also included the information to purchase tickets to the festival. All I had to do was follow the links and put down my money, which took all of five minutes.

With some hesitation at the ease of booking the trip, I closed the laptop. Charlie put his head in my lap and looked up at me, his signal that he had to go outside. I stood from the table and let him out the sliding glass door into the backyard. A warm breeze drifted across the overgrown field into the dining room. My nostrils were filled with the sweet smells of summer. Instinctively, I scanned the field looking for little grey monsters stalking me from the shadows, waiting for another opportunity to snatch me out of my house.

Charlie walked through the door back into the house and I stood there peering into the night. There was nothing unusual out there that I could see. I paused for another moment before closing the sliding door. If I had one wish it was to never see those things again.

Exhausted, I walked up the stairs and my faithful dog followed me. Our paths split as I walked into the bathroom and he veered off into the bedroom. As I brushed my teeth I looked in the mirror. My face looked better than before, but I still felt like a shell of a person. The essence of who I was before the abduction was gone. There was no more light in my eyes, only the dull reflection of defeat.

I walked out of the bathroom, passed through the hall, and stared into my bedroom. The space was bathed in the light of a half moon, most everything visible, but some things remained hidden in the shadows. That was where the monsters could hide until I was fast asleep. A shiver ran through me as I considered the implications of sleeping there that night. Nothing was different than any other night since I'd been taken away, except that I was different. From his bed on the floor, Charlie raised his head as I walked into the room, grabbed my pillow and comforter off the bed, and walked back through the door.

Sensing that the sleeping arrangements had changed my dog followed me downstairs and into the living room. He made fast work of working out a spot on the area rug to lie down. I ignored his instinctual routine and set up my bed on the sofa. I wrapped myself in the comforter and pressed my head into the pillow. Wind blew through the creaky old eaves of the house. There was no way I could fall asleep listening to that.

Instead of cowering under the covers and waiting for things of the night to creep toward me, I reached out to the coffee table, grabbed the remote, and turned on the television. The flat screen sprang to life with all of its plastic people and places on display. I turned the volume down to a murmur, faced the back of the sofa and fell asleep.

● ● ●

The next day at work I asked my boss for some time off. He said yes without any hesitation. The vacation plans progressed with such ease that I felt the universe or whatever you want to call it was paving the way for this trip. In the past, I'd used most of my vacation time to catch up with work on the farm, which didn't amount to much since there was no farming that took place there. I hoped that I'd have some time to try to relax and think far away from home.

Work on that day and the days that followed were torture. I spent most of my time dreading the perimeter checks once the sun went down and the shadows grew long. I skipped about half of my scheduled rounds. It was a good thing there was no one there to care or take notice.

When I did make the rounds, I walked faster than I should have and always looked straight ahead of me, or toward the next corner of the building. The forest that surrounded the fruit processing plant did not exist in my mind during the darkness of night. I clutched my heavy Maglite flashlight tight as both a source of light and as a possible weapon. If needed, I could always brain someone or something over the head with it.

I avoided looking up, especially on clear nights. If my eyes stayed focused on the ground there was no way I'd see anything with dull metal and spinning lights. It would be near impossible for anything unusual to notice me if I just kept my head buried in sand. And just like that, I recognized my fear of open spaces.

Then again, nearly everything had terrified me since this whole thing began. I was a new creature, a fearful one, and if I wasn't careful I would turn into a recluse and shut out the world altogether. That was not what I wanted for my life. Yet, somehow I was alone. It hadn't happened all at once, but developed over time until I never saw anyone outside of absolute necessity. The last person that was a real part of my life was my sister, who'd abandoned me after trying countless times to convince me to sell the house and the farm. When was the last time I'd heard from her?

Headlights in the distance beyond the guard shack pulled me out of my thoughts. As they grew closer, I realized it was Alicia, the closest thing I had to a true friend. I opened the gate and met her outside. The car door flew open so fast I thought it might fly off its hinges.

Alicia beamed. "I can't believe you're going all the way to New Mexico. It's so exciting and spontaneous. I'd give anything to go with you."

"I wish I could take someone with me, but I need to do this by myself. It's not just a pleasure cruise and I'm not sure how much fun I would be. But if there was someone I could take, it would be you."

She smiled at me. "I just think it's so cool. You'll have to tell me all about it. And don't worry about Charlie. We'll take good care of him."

I tensed up, knowing that I should tell her the whole reason for the trip. That stubborn old block prevented me from sharing the sordid tale. Maybe I would spill my guts when I got back into town, and then again maybe I'd just go run and jump in front of a speeding train.

"You know I'll tell you all about it," was as far as I could go.

● ● ●

I spent another restless night on the couch in my living room. I knew it was silly to think that no harm could come to me if I slept anywhere but my bedroom. Still, there was some comfort in the little nest I'd made for myself. Charlie adapted as well and slept in his own space on the area rug.

I drifted off to sleep thinking about Carla and the rest of the Avondale Paranormal Society. I decided to hold off on telling any of them about my plans to visit the UFO Festival in Roswell, and my intention to meet and speak with Dr. Lincoln. Carla's negative reaction was more than enough incentive to keep that information to myself.

• 15 •

I discovered another fear to add to the growing list, and like the others, it was one I did not expect; the fear of flying. I hadn't thought much about it, especially since Alicia did all the planning, but I'd never flown anywhere before. Granted, the fear of being crammed into a metal tube with wings and racing through the sky was rather common compared to the fear of being abducted by aliens, but my throat went dry and my hands felt clammy just the same.

As instructed by the confirmation email, I arrived at the airport two hours ahead of schedule. I parked in a lot about a half mile away from the relatively small airport outside Avondale. The sound of a plane taking off greeted me as I stepped out of the truck. I ducked out of instinct and felt my body start to tremble. In an attempt to alleviate my anxiety I watched the plane climb higher into the sky. It didn't explode mid-air but just kept on going higher and further away. That was a good sign.

I grabbed my wheeled carry-on and backpack

from the bed of the truck and walked a short distance to the shuttle stop. A family of four waited next to a metal bench with all their gear. Based on the age of the kids and the lack of enthusiasm on the faces of the parents, I guessed they were headed to sunny Florida and the wonders of Disney World. I smiled and set my bag down on the ground.

The shuttle pulled up and the driver put the luggage in the cargo area. The kids rushed to the back of the large van, and the parents ambled in after them. I was about to climb into the front seat when a few more people arrived. An elderly couple told a woman dressed in a pantsuit and heels that they were traveling to California to visit family, and the smart dressed woman let them know she was headed to New York City on business. Everyone was all smiles as they piled into the van. I tried hard to focus on their combined enthusiasm but felt the gnawing pit in my stomach grow bigger.

By all rights, flying is considered the safest form of travel. It is also the most terrifying should something go wrong. The words *No Survivors* were plastered across the front page of the newspaper in my head. I imagined dangling oxygen masks, blow up lifejackets, and seats to be used as floatation devices, which were nice things to temper the shared dread of a sudden loss of cabin pressure and subsequent plunge toward the earth. My seat would do me no good as a life preserver since there were no large bodies of water between Avondale and Roswell, and it would do little to cushion a fall into trees, rocks, and dirt.

When the shuttle arrived at the terminal, I grabbed my belongings, gave the driver a tip and did my best to calm my nerves as I walked toward the automatic swinging doors of the Avondale Municipal Airport. As I stepped inside, I looked left and right. There were only a handful of airlines in the terminal. I checked the sign for mine, and then remembered that I had printed my boarding pass. I also had no luggage to check and no reason to visit one of the perky workers behind the long counter.

I heard the heels of the woman headed to New York City click against the hard floor with purpose. I followed her to a short line where TSA Agents, metal detectors, total body scanners, and conveyor belts waited to detect and weed out the dangerous passengers.

I took my place and line and turned back to see the family on their way to the land of sun and hurricanes struggling with their own luggage. The young boy and girl wore the bright smiles of youth while the parents dragged behind, looking exhausted before they had even begun.

The short line for security took longer than expected. I shuffled along at a turtles pace with the rest of the passengers. Most tolerated the inconvenience of having to pass through such a strict security processing assembly line with the thinnest of patience. It seemed they had forgotten the event that had started all of this paranoid focus on passenger screening. 9/11 had already become a ghost of the past despite the fact that the fee named for it was paid on every single plane ticket.

As I approached the unsmiling TSA screening agent, I watched a man who stood a short distance away from two uniformed men who searched through his belongings. He looked at me, rolled his eyes, and crossed his arms. In another area, a woman stood inside a total body scanner with her arms held up high and behind her head as the machinery circled her. It looked like she was being arrested.

"Your ticket and ID, sir," the flat faced female

TSA agent barked. She looked like a person whose bad side I wanted to avoid at all costs. The tight bun on the top of her head seemed to stretch all the expression from her pinched face.

I handed her my boarding pass and ID and gave her a smile. She never made eye contact with me, and only glanced up once to confirm that the picture matched the person. She waved me through and I took the few steps toward a stack of empty plastic bins at the base of the conveyor belt. I put my carry on and backpack on the belt, fished my keys and cell phone out of my pocket and placed them in a bin. I was just about to walk into the full body scanner when a burly male TSA agent stopped me.

"You have to take off your shoes, sir. Please step back and place them in a bin."

His tone was not accusatory but had an edge to it that made me feel guilty anyway. I took off my shoes, placed them in a plastic bin, and stepped back into the full body scanner line. The sophisticated piece of machinery looked like nothing more than one of those wind machines I'd seen in the mall, where they manufacture the wind of a hurricane for some sort of adrenaline rush. And all for just five bucks.

A heavyset bald man walked into the contraption ahead of me. He stepped into the body scanner and put his arms up. It was hard not to notice the sweat stains in his armpits. I checked mine to make sure they weren't moist.

After the man left the platform, I was waved into the machine. On the floor, there was a diagram to tell me where to place my feet, as well as another one on the wall to show me how to raise my arms. The thought crossed my mind that the person watching the monitor may be able to see more of me than I wanted them to, but it was already too late to protest. In any case, the only other option was a full body pat down, and that sounded like a nightmare in comparison.

The scan was over in seconds. I stepped out, gathered my belongings and trudged my way to the gate. I sat in the waiting area and tried to take my mind off the impending flight. That proved difficult considering I was sitting in the middle of an airport waiting to board my plane. The screening process had taken just under half an hour. Ninety minutes was too much time to contemplate everything that could go wrong on the flight.

I had the sudden thought that flying thirty thousand or so feet in the air would put me even closer to the dark skies my tormentors descended from. I shivered and wondered if the fear I felt was evident on my face. No one seemed to notice my internal struggle. My poker face was strong.

Time passed slowly, but it did pass. A plane taxied to the gate and a few minutes later people poured out of the exit. Most looked weary from travel. A few wore genuine smiles of contentment. I imagined that the happy people were on vacation, or reuniting with loved ones they hadn't seen in a long time, and the weary ones were returning home. Of course, it could be just the opposite for some of those people, but it was easier to generalize than to get caught up in all the potential scenarios.

A few minutes after everyone deboarded the plane, a ticketing agent stepped up to the desk and started typing into the computer. My hands felt clammy again and my throat was bone dry. Logic tried to convince me not to be afraid, but my irrational fear center did not allow me any relief from the anxiety. My stomach churned.

I boarded the plane without incident and even

made my way to my seat in the aisle with relative ease. Once I was settled, I leaned over to close the plastic shade at the window seat and hoped for a fellow passenger who had no desire to look out and admire the world from so far above. I put my earbuds in and listened to some music in an attempt to distract myself.

The plane filled up fast. I ended up sitting next to a girl who looked about eight years old and her mother. My hopes dashed, the young girl immediately opened the window and looked out at the tarmac. The mother sat watching her daughter, commenting as well on the wonders of what they saw outside the window. I closed my eyes and tilted my head back.

I was fine until the plane stopped taxiing into position and prepared for takeoff. Everyone grew strangely quiet as the engines revved and the plane began to move forward. The lights in the cabin flickered and there was a sickening swaying motion as the metal tube gained speed. The roar of the engines filled the cabin with a sound like loud static. A few seconds later the plane left the ground and climbed into the sky.

I gripped the armrests so tight that my hands cramped. At some point, I had closed my eyes and dared not to open them until I was certain the plane had not exploded. I swallowed a lump that had formed in my throat and was grateful I had decided not to eat anything that morning.

It took a little while to get used to the ride, and somehow I managed to sleep for much of the three-hour flight to Roswell. I assumed it was from the utter exhaustion of being so tense that my body shut down. It also kept me from answering uncomfortable questions from well-meaning passengers.

When the plane bounced onto the tarmac in

Roswell, I was certain it was going to veer off course into the desert beyond, hit a bump, flip, and burst into a ball of fire. It didn't. We landed safely and I breathed for what felt like the first time since passing through the doors of my hometown airport a few hours earlier.

Another wave of anxiety washed over me as we pulled up to the gate. I wanted nothing more than to get out of the bullet train in the sky and set my feet on a solid surface. The wait was excruciating as one row after another exited the plane. As soon as I walked out of the gate I marveled at the landscape beyond the windows. There was nothing but miles and miles of barren desert punctuated by mountains in the distance. I was not used to that sort of desolation. And yet, there I was in Roswell, New Mexico.

• 16 •

I arrived a day ahead of the UFO Festival hoping to
avoid the majority of the crowd. A good number of
visitors had the same idea. In the baggage claim area
of the airport, people wore colorful T-shirts depicting a
variety of alien faces, a few had put on masks to cover
their faces, and one person sat on a bench beside a full
body alien costume wrapped in plastic. Most wore smiles
and were engaged in light conversation. No one seemed
to take any of it seriously.

I had no need to wait for any bags and walked
past them to pick up my car rental. A wave of heat rushed
over me as I exited the building to pick up the econobox
I'd be driving the next few days. It was hard to believe I
was really there in Roswell. The tarmac of the airport
parking lot shimmered with the heat adding to the already
surreal environment. The temperature felt hotter than I
expected, but not nearly as suffocating as the sweltering,
humid dog days of summer back home. Either way, hot
was hot. I stuffed myself into the car, turned the key to

start it up, and cranked the air conditioning.

I decided to take the longer route to my hotel at the north end of Roswell. Just outside the airport, I was struck by the sparse vegetation and the scorched, sun-bleached look of the industrial buildings along the way. I drove through several residential and industrial sections of the city before hitting the outskirts of the town proper.

I passed a sign that declared Roswell to be the dairy capital of the southwest – a factoid I found troubling for a reason I couldn't explain – just before seeing another sign advertising the Roswell International Museum and Research Center. A chill crept down my neck as I thought about the 'research' that was conducted on me by my abductors from another world. I resolved to avoid the museum at all costs.

I drove by a streetlamp that had two large alien eye decals plastered onto its face. I wondered if the people who lived there and visited had any idea what kind of creatures they were dealing with. The frivolous way the images of those beasts were splashed around town made it apparent that there were few people who knew how dangerous the aliens really were.

Several shops along the way advertised all things UFO and alien. I made a pact with myself not to enter any of them. A short time later, I passed a McDonalds built to look like a spaceship. I couldn't help but chuckle in disbelief at the silliness of it all. If I hadn't been paralyzed and tortured by the creatures the people of that town worshipped, I might have been able to laugh it off myself. But I was the buzz kill at the party; the only one awake while everyone else slept.

Just outside the downtown area, I passed the New Mexico Military Institute. Like much of Roswell, the architecture was institutional and box-like, its contents shrouded in mystery. I felt a heaviness in the air, something almost spiritual in nature. I was disturbed not only by the festival, but by the attitudes of some of the people I'd seen so far and the willingness of the collective mob to participate in the worship of unknown gods.

Beyond the military institute, there were several hotels and motels, along with just about every national restaurant chain available. My already dry throat felt scorched as I continued driving, and I realized that my hands were wet with perspiration despite the air conditioning pumping out of the vents. I looked into the rearview mirror and noticed my forehead was wet as well. I wondered if coming to Roswell was a mistake.

I checked into the Comfort Inn and Suites on North Main Street without much fanfare. I took the access cards from the clerk and continued into the interior of the hotel. I was trembling by the time I entered my room, and could not admire the modern and functional design with just the right touch of southwestern flair to make it comfortable. I double locked the door behind me and headed straight to the bathroom to release my bowels.

After washing my hands, I splashed cold water on my face and focused on breathing. It was a struggle to maintain my composure as I walked out of the bathroom and headed straight toward the bed. I plopped down onto it face down and felt instantly exhausted. My trip had just started and I was already whipped. Dr. Lincoln would not be in Roswell until day two of the festival, and I had to somehow make it until then without turning into a blubbering useless puddle of nerves.

I decided the best thing to do was to take a nap. I closed the block-out curtains and cranked the air conditioning as cold as it would go. Soon, I drifted off into a dreamless sleep with no intention of waking early.

● ● ●

It was late afternoon when I first arrived in Roswell. I woke from my nap with a jolt in complete darkness. No light leaked around the edges of the curtains. It was impossible to believe I had slept for so long.

To provide some ambient light, I switched on the bedside lamp and jumped back. The big green head of an alien with the signature large black eyes and expressionless slit for a mouth reflected off the mirror from a festival brochure on the desk. I gave a nervous laugh, not because anything was funny, but because I could either laugh or cry, and laughing seemed like the better option.

I pulled back the curtain to view the landscape beyond the window, and it was just as desolate at night as during the day. The only exception was the haze of light pollution that was present above every populated area in the United States. I crossed my arms and looked out the glass at the Hampton Inn and Suites nearby. A few of the windows were lit, but most were dark. The festival revelers slept in preparation to celebrate the worship orgy for their alien gods.

I stepped back into the room, wondering if I was being too judgmental. I could see myself laughing at, or even partaking in all the hoopla of the UFO Festival before my own experience. But armed with at least a portion of the truth I knew that people were pouring out adoration to creatures bent on torturing humans.

I looked around the room and felt a sudden restlessness. The car keys on the nightstand beckoned to me, and I felt an urge to drive into downtown Roswell. As I turned to look out the window at the soft glowing lights of the city, a surge of anxiety quenched my wanderlust and I decided to visit the pool and hot tub in the hotel instead.

To my surprise, the pool and hot tub were housed in a sheltered indoor area. It was clean, with a non-offensive rectangular pool and square hot tub. It took a moment to decide if I wanted to swim in the cool water, or kick back and relax in the warm water and soothing jets. I went for the hot tub. As I submerged my body, I marveled at the idea that it was probably cooler in the pool room of the hotel than it was outside. The only other people were a couple of kids that played in the pool and a woman who sat on a lounge chair reading a paperback. I leaned back and closed my eyes, desperate to allow the water to melt away my stress.

I nearly drifted off to sleep while soaking in the near scorching water. It was the first time I'd felt a moment of relaxation since arriving in Roswell. I started to believe that my vacation could have moments of pleasure in between episodes of terror. Enjoyment was one thing my family could never afford, at least not by cultural standards. As I may have mentioned earlier, our vacations were in our own backyard and rarely fun.

The jets stopped pushing the water around me and I opened my eyes to an empty pool area. The woman reading her book and the playing children were gone. I was used to the solitude that comes from living in the country with far-flung neighbors, but there was something odd about being alone in a public area of a hotel. The unfamiliar emotion of loneliness crept into my consciousness. Why was I always alone?

There was no time to contemplate the question. I had just stepped out of the hot tub and wrapped myself in a towel when a group of four teenagers – two boys and two girls – entered the area with raucous laughter. I envied their ability to laugh, to be freely alive without the comprehension of the fragility of life. I glared at them, feeling unfair resentment at their carefree attitude. As they passed by me on the way to the pool, one of the boys pushed a girl into the pool, and she splashed hard into the water. The rest of the group laughed and dove in after her.

I walked out of the pool area, allowing the echoes of their good time to fade away behind me. It was hard to remember when I had enjoyed life last, just for its own sake. The closest I came was when my sister and I held down the farm together. It was short-lived, and she constantly wanted to sell.

My stubborn refusal to move on and get my own life had driven her away. If I had one thing to do over again, I'd sell the farm and we'd take off together and start a new life somewhere else. But she was gone and thinking about changing the past brought nothing but pain and regret.

As soon as I entered my room, I changed into a solid black T-shirt and a pair of khaki cargo shorts. I knew it would probably be best to go to sleep, but my long nap earlier in the day stopped me. Wide awake, I took a few steps toward the window, leaned my body against the glass, and looked out at the city lights once more. Those stupid lights both called to me and made me want to stay right where I was. I was curious about venturing into danger but too afraid to take that step. I knew, or at least hoped, that nothing I would find in this tourist Mecca was likely to harm me, but the logical part of my brain had lost much of its control long ago.

Unwilling to succumb to my fear, I slipped on a pair of faded black flip flops, grabbed my wallet, keycard, and car keys off the side table, and made my way through the hotel into the parking lot. I paused for a moment, struck by the stars burning bright in the western sky. There were no clouds and the clarity of the atmosphere was remarkable. I turned my head toward the heavens and marveled at the vast expanse of space above me. It was so big, and I was so small. I'd seen the stars like that back home, but it was rare for the sky to be so clear and crisp. The clean sky above the desert created an almost holographic effect, making the stars feel closer. I resisted the urge to reach out and touch them.

I continued the short walk to the car and contorted myself into the miniature bucket seat. If I had it to do over again, I'd have reserved a regular sized car, or an SUV, or anything else. It was hard to believe anyone drove a little car like that on purpose. I sat inside with the air conditioning blasting for a few moments before determining in my mind to drive as far as the Roswell International Museum and Research Center.

The drive took less time at night with no traffic. I passed the same assorted shops now lit up with neon signs and illuminated plastic alien figures that stood guard outside the doors. The spaceship-shaped McDonald's was glaringly bright with a variety of colored lights that streamed across its surface. And despite my earlier revulsion at the garish display of alien worship, I had to admit that there was something amusing about the cartoonish way everything appeared at night. I even cracked a smile.

Just past the museum on Main Street, I saw a grey figure with black, soulless eyes standing at a bus stop by the side of the road. It was unnerving to see the creature illuminated by the harsh overhead streetlight. I clenched the wheel tighter and held my breath as I slowed down. Its eyes seemed to follow me as I drove past, and I fought the urge to scream. I continued driving forward and looked in the rearview mirror just in time to watch it wrench at its neck and take its head off, revealing a human head underneath. It was a teenage kid in a costume. I let out a ragged breath.

My mind leapt to thinking that it would be an ingenious idea for the real thing to hide among the revelers who only pretended to be monsters. They could come and go as they pleased, soaking up the adoration from their sycophantic fans without ever being recognized for the monsters they were. I wondered if they had feelings, whether they craved attention or adoration, or if they just liked inflicting pain and observing the suffering of humans.

At the end of Main Street, I turned around and drove back to the hotel. I saw the kid in the alien costume on the way back. He was smiling and talking excitedly with a man and woman he stood with. I assumed they were his parents. What kind of people condoned participation in the celebration of aliens? I know my parents never would have allowed me to go to some UFO festival. Then again, it was a different world from the one I grew up in.

As I passed them, I noticed dad wore a black shirt with a bright orange alien on the front with the words 'Take me to Your Leader' written underneath it. Mom wore a white shirt with an image of Earth with an arrow pointing up that said *Outer Space is my Home*. I shook my head and drove on.

It was hard to be objective and simply say that the people who attended the festival were just having a good time and no harm was being done. The fact that monsters were being celebrated in this way made me want to shake someone and slap them awake from their self-imposed stupor. Maybe if I started acting crazy like that I would fit right in with the rest of them.

Further down the road, a small group of people stood in front of a bookstore. One of the men held a huge wooden cross with white rope lights lining its border. A teenage boy held a cardboard sign that read 'Repent and be Saved'. A woman in the group held an open bible and read something from it that I could not hear. A little girl with them waved at me as I passed by. I smiled back at her.

The wackos were already out, and I imagined it would only get worse as the festival progressed. I wondered how much I'd be able to tolerate. But this and so much more was what I signed up for. It was my own fault that I was stuck in this desert place with nowhere to go and nothing to do but join in the festivities, or further seclude myself from civilization.

● ● ●

I chose seclusion on the first day of the festival and decided to visit one of the places Alicia suggested, Bottomless Lakes State Park. There were plenty of swimming holes where I was from, but how often would the opportunity to go swimming in a lake in the middle of the desert present itself?

The bad news was that I had to endure the drive back through the middle of downtown Roswell before heading east on Second Avenue for another ten miles or so to get to the park. As I expected, the sidewalks were jammed with plenty of tourists willing to spend hours combing through alien merchandise and phony recreations of UFO sightings, abductions, and alien autopsies.

I was relieved to leave it all behind as I drove away from downtown, seeking refuge from the chaos. It wasn't long before the only structures I saw were power lines stretched between gigantic metal towers that resembled Baphomet heads. With the vast expanses of wind scraped sand, it was hard to believe there was an end to the desolation.

A few minutes later, I reached the gate to Bottomless Lake State Park. The major attraction, Lea Lake, was at the southernmost end of the park. I drove straight past the other sections, and looked forward to the idea of seeing people having some non-alien oriented fun.

The lack of trees and the sheer openness of the land in the park and surrounding area was hard to comprehend. Shade was sparse and the hot sun baked everything in sight. I was used to being surrounded by thick shade trees that formed a natural canopy to protect my fragile skin.

A gentle rise at the furthest reaches of my vision revealed layers of enchanting multi-colored rock. I had a fleeting moment where I wondered if I should have gone camping instead of booking a hotel.

My daydream about camping in the desert changed the instant I opened the door. The heat blasted my face like a furnace and took my breath away. I grabbed my sunscreen and towel off the passenger seat, stepped out of the car, and headed to the beach area.

A squat cliff rose on one side of Lea Lake, giving it a dramatic backdrop. A rather large structure with covered picnic tables surrounded the swimming area in a semicircle. Within it, there was a small snack shop and a counter to rent paddleboats and kayaks.

I had expected the park to be more crowded, considering that there were probably not many places to swim in New Mexico, but it wasn't too bad. There were less than two dozen families scattered around the beach; enough to make me not feel so alone, but not so many that it was overcrowded.

I set my towel down on the beach and stripped off my T-shirt. As I stepped out of my sandals, the sun-scorched sand set my feet on fire. I raced toward the water, hoping for some refuge from the unrelenting heat burning my poor feet. I didn't even have time to think before I dove into the clear water. I was surprised by two things. The first was just how cold the water felt against my skin. The second was that when I came up just a few feet from shore, I could not touch the bottom. They didn't call them the bottomless lakes for nothing.

I swam the short distance to the edge of the beach and pulled myself up onto the hot sand. I was covered in goosebumps and actually shivered despite the mind-numbing heat of the air. It was difficult to reconcile the idea that such extremes in temperature could coexist in one place.

On the beach, I looked around and realized there were not many people actually swimming in the water. Some children stayed close to shore splashing in the shallow end and built sand castles, but most of the people in the lake were on some sort of flotation device or another. I lacked the foresight for that kind of preparation.

I dove back into the lake. The cool water rushed over me and my senses were exhilarated by the cleansing effect of the frigid temperature. After another plunge, I decided to rest for a few minutes. I lay down on my towel and welcomed the warmth it offered after being in water so cold hypothermia could have set in. And all this in the middle of the desert. Maybe God or the universe had a sense of humor after all.

I closed my eyes and allowed myself to relax. The sun flared down on my flesh, and I knew I would not be able to tolerate the intense heat for much longer before turning into a lobster. It was the middle of summer and I had a pretty good tan from working out in the yard, but this was too much for my northern skin. I slipped on my flip-flops, grabbed my towel and headed to the covered picnic area.

I sat at a table facing the lake and observed the laziness of the activity in the park. People were there, but everyone moved in slow motion. Time seemed to stand still, stretched somehow. It was as if the world outside no longer existed and I was on my own abandoned island. It was a place where the schemes of men or the devil had no room to thrive. It was just me and myself.

I hadn't planned on it but decided to rent a kayak for an hour to explore a little bit of the lake. I walked back to my car to grab my wallet. I paid a small deposit to a shirtless pimple-faced boy at the shop and was out exploring in no time at all. The water was so still that the only disruption was from the ripple of my oar. There was also a bizarre magnification effect that made fifty feet look like five. The lake appeared shallow but was far deeper than anyone would have guessed.

My hour was up far too soon. I returned the kayak and spent the rest of the afternoon under the picnic shelter gazing at the tranquility of the lake. Every few minutes I closed my eyes and listened to the white noise of the soft breeze accented with the occasional sounds of talking and laughter of other people in the distance. The over-baked smell of everything in the desert filled my nostrils. I felt peace for the first time in months.

A man, woman, and two small children sat down at a table a few rows down from me. The man, shirtless and red as a lobster, pulled some sandwiches, juice boxes, and a couple of sodas out of a well-worn cooler. He passed one out to the woman and each of the kids. They all paused and he prayed over their meager meal. It was a simple request for a simple blessing. Something my family never did.

The man asked what the kids' favorite part of the day was so far. The words the boy spoke first drove a dagger through my heart. "I like being here at the lake with you and Mommy."

His words stuck with me. Had I ever felt that way about my own family, just enjoying and appreciating their presence without any further expectation? My dad, mom, me, and even my sister prided ourselves on our independent spirits, but we always seemed to end up alone; craving human connection, but creating isolation instead.

I stayed at the park until the sun faded into the horizon. The park ranger had to tell me it was time to leave. While reluctant to lose the magic of a perfect day of relaxation, I knew there was work to be done and truth to be explored out in this barren wasteland.

I slumped into the driver seat of my rental car and

sighed, wishing the day was not at an end. The park ranger closed the gate behind me as I exited the park and turned left. Each mile closer to Roswell brought back the tension and anxiety my day away from reality had cured. My muscles tightened as I approached Main Street. The lights of the city blazed as bright as the night before, but instead of a few scattered alien worshippers, there was representation of every imaginable variation of extraterrestrial life.

My breathing became shallow and fast. Low-level panic spread from my chest to my arms and wormed its way into my hands. I gripped the steering wheel hard and forced myself to focus on the road ahead of me. Beads of perspiration formed on my forehead despite the air conditioning rushing out of the vents. My heart skipped to its own beat. I fought the urge to scream as the green light ahead of me turned yellow, then red.

Streams of people dressed as monsters from other worlds passed in front of my car at the intersection. A bright green rubber alien hand smacked against the top of my hood. I jumped in my seat and stared into the empty eye sockets of a bright green oversized alien head. The creature had apparently lost its balance and reached out to stop itself from falling. After regaining composure the alien bobbed its head and waved at me with a big bright green hand. I gave an uneasy smile in return.

To stop myself from hyperventilating, I forced myself to take deep breaths. By the time the light turned green I was trembling all over. It was a white-knuckle ride to the hotel as I endured an endless barrage of costumed people inhabiting every corner of the area near the convention center. Somehow, I made it to the hotel parking lot without passing out. Fighting back tears, I grabbed my bag from the car and dashed across the parking lot toward the lobby. I could make out the glow of the lights from the city, and multiple searchlights cutting back and forth across the sky through my blurred vision. I shuddered as I passed through the lobby door and almost ran toward the elevator.

It took far too long to make it to my room. I struggled to stick the keycard into the slot. Once the door was unlocked, I flung it open as fast as I could and locked it behind me. I took a few ragged breaths and rushed into the bathroom, closing and locking that door as well. A few seconds later, I was sitting in the dry bathtub, hugging myself and rocking back and forth. I didn't know how I was going to get through the next day, but there was no way I would miss Dr. Lincoln.

• 17 •

My sleep that night was disrupted by nightmares. In the most vivid, one of the grey aliens took me captive and paraded me through the streets of Roswell like some sort of trophy. People dressed in costumes whooped and hollered as I was led down that street toward a bright beam of light that descended from a hovering spaceship. I was paralyzed and unable to plead for help or warn anyone else to run away for the sake of their own souls. I woke up panting, and wished more than anything else that I could go home to my illusion of safety.

Despite my severe exhaustion and sour mood, I showered, shaved, and dressed in a new pair of cargo shorts and a black t-shirt. I contemplated eating something from the continental breakfast, but my churning stomach would not allow it. I grabbed a cup of coffee to go and a banana for later.

The drive into downtown that morning was quiet. A few stragglers populated the streets here and there, but for the most part, the nighttime revelers were confined to their rooms, sleeping off the good time from the day before. I was glad Dr. Lincoln was scheduled to speak at 9:00 am.

I parked my car in an overpriced lot as close as possible and took a short walk to the convention center. The lull in the activity of the festival helped me to have the courage to do what I came to do. Just inside the doors, small crowds gathered for the various exhibits and presentations scheduled for that morning. Some people were dressed in costume, but most were in plain clothes, smiling and carefree. I envied them for their ignorance.

The room Dr. Lincoln was booked into was slightly bigger than a janitor's closet. The sign outside was an 8 x 10 piece of cheap white copier paper with a simple black font that read, *What are these aliens among us?* Chairs were packed into the tiny space as tight as possible, with a small raised platform and projector screen at the front. Our host was nowhere to be found. I took a seat in a back corner, hoping to blend into the background which was impossible due to the intimacy of the space.

Several people wandered in after me, but not more than ten or so. I wasn't sure if that was a good or bad sign. I didn't have long to wait long to find out.

Dr. Ron Lincoln walked in a few minutes later, carrying a laptop case and a well-worn binder with a notebook that had assorted loose papers sticking out of it. I guessed he was in his fifties due to his mostly grey hair, full beard, and mustache. He wore jeans and a blue button-up shirt with a brown corduroy jacket, reminiscent of a tenured second-rate community college professor. He avoided eye contact with everyone as he walked the short distance to the front of the room.

It took Dr. Lincoln several minutes to connect his

laptop to the projector and gather his notes. With clicker in hand, he stepped up onto the platform and started his presentation. "Thank you all for coming out." He scanned the audience and it was hard to tell if he was disappointed by such a low turnout.

"I'm not here to entertain you, or bore you with weak attempts at humor. I am here to simply inform you of what I believe UFO's, aliens, and most supernatural phenomena really are based on countless hours of research and personal experience."

By this point, I realized his style was direct, without fluff or fanfare.

Dr. Lincoln cleared his throat, pointed his clicker, and an image of a typical grey alien popped up on the screen behind him. "UFO's and little grey men are not spaceships or creatures from other planets sent to Earth to display their glory or kidnap humans for innocuous research. They are a part of the overall Luciferian deception. Abductions are nothing more than the work of demons; an attempt to distract us from the truth. The same is true of ghosts and a host of other 'otherworldly' activity that many so-called experts have such difficulty explaining."

Demons? Could UFO's and alien abductions be the works of demons, as in Satan's little helpers? My head spun as I tried to consider the idea. I wasn't sure what I had expected Dr. Lincoln to say, but that was not it.

A new slide of a black bodied demonic creature with red eyes filled the screen. "Demons exist in a dimension outside of our own and have the ability to see into and manipulate ours. Think of it as a sort of special effect or visual illusion."

A young red-haired man with silver glasses interrupted. "Oh come on, doctor. Even if I can accept

UFO sightings as elaborate special effects designed by creatures in another dimension, how can I be expected to accept that the experience of alien abduction is nothing more than a hallucination?"

Dr. Lincoln looked directly at the young man for a half a second before continuing. "I am about to answer that question. Before I go on, I do have to ask the audience to hold questions until the end. Most of them will be answered by the time I am finished."

No one said anything further.

"Along with having influence over the atmosphere in our environment, demons also have the ability to create false memories for those who are not protected by grace."

False memories? Impossible. I knew that what had happened to me that day a few months ago was as real as the cheap plastic seat my butt was parked in. I shifted, crossed my arms, and considered marching out of the room. There was no way my abduction was nothing more than a false memory.

Dr. Lincoln continued. "We only need to look at the various accounts of UFO and alien sightings over the last fifty years to see the variation in the look and feel of the technology used by these creatures. Over the decades, the first-hand accounts of these so-called 'abductions' matched those depicted in books, film, and television. The technology 'evolved' right along with our imagined vision of the future. There is one constant, and that is the creatures themselves, commonly referred to as 'The Greys'."

A lump formed in my throat as my mind fought against the idea. I was either the subject of extraterrestrial or demonic experimentation and torture. Neither option was good.

"'The Greys' are not confined to descriptions of alien lifeforms. As early as the 1600's there are reports of people who were known to be demon possessed providing descriptions of short, grey, hairless creatures, with huge black eyes that would 'take them away' from their normal surroundings and torture them. But back then, 'The Greys' were called by their true name."

My mind had just barely accepted the concept that I was whisked away and tormented by aliens. Now, I was expected to believe that it was not creatures from another galaxy, but from another dimension, possibly from the very depths of hell.

"And not only that. The common experience of a modern-day alien abduction matches that of a seventeenth-century case of demonic oppression or possession with the primary difference being the setting of the torture. There were no ideas of spaceships back then."

The projector switched to a drawing of a demon described by a subject in 1684. It had horns, fangs, and a look of malice. It was not at all like the aliens I'd seen. An older couple to the right of me got up from their chairs and left, shaking their heads as they walked the short distance to the door.

Dr. Lincoln eyed them as they walked away, but continued as if nothing had happened at all. "The people who are the targets of demonic oppression and possession are not accidental. In most cases, the people have welcomed these entities into their lives through occult practices, left themselves open to demonic attack by denying the truth of grace, or are part of a generational bloodline curse."

The red-haired rabble-rouser with the silver glasses got up and left along with three others. The look on the doctor's face remained unchanged, as if he was accustomed to this type of rejection. I stayed right where I was, unable to move. His line about generational curses led me to thoughts about my grandfather.

There were only two other people in the room, but Dr. Lincoln continued as if he was speaking to a full house. "In a strange twist, the only confirmed way to stop the sightings and abductions is the name of Jesus. Multiple witnesses have reported success in using the name of Jesus, but unless they put their faith in Jesus permanently, the demons return. My theory is that once a person truly accepts Jesus as Lord and Savior, the Holy Spirit intercedes to defend that person from the evil ones."

The only other person in the room rose from her chair and walked out the door. It was just the two of us. Myself and Dr. Lincoln. Only then did he look disappointed.

Instead of continuing his presentation, he looked at me directly. "Well young man, do you have any questions?" After he asked the question, he muttered under his breath, "every year I lose more and more..."

There were rumblings of questions in my brain, but nothing solid. He motioned for me to move closer. I got up and walked to the first row. The projector blinked off, and he stepped off the small stage and took a seat beside me.

Dr. Lincoln removed his glasses and turned toward me. "Tell me, young man, what's your story?"

I could tell he was interested in what I had to say in a way that was similar to Alicia's curiosity, but different, more clinical then whimsical. "Well, Dr. Lincoln. My name is Alex."

He waved his glasses at me and crossed his legs.

"Please, just call me Ron. That doctor business is so pretentious, but necessary on some occasions."

I almost laughed out loud, but restrained myself. "Ok, Ron. It's a long story, and I'm not very good at telling stories, so please be patient with me."

Dr. Lincoln, or Ron, nodded his head, encouraging me to continue.

Once I started talking about my experiences I could not stop. Everything spilled out. And not just the sightings and abduction. My fear of being alone for the rest of my life, and my deep worry that I would end up like my crazy grandpa, and what felt like a thousand other things ran like vomit out of my mouth. He just sat and listened, nodding his head and responding when appropriate.

It was a good long while before I stopped talking. There was an extended period of silence while I waited for a reaction, anything to break the awkwardness of the moment. When he finally spoke, it startled me.

"Well, Alex, that is quite a harrowing tale. Do you remember what I said earlier about how to stop all this from happening?"

I nodded my head yes, swallowing the lump in my throat. His words had a strange effect on me, like a pulling sensation, an ache for something I longed for, but could not put into words. I reasoned that it could also be my empty stomach with all the acids swirling about. My head throbbed and an ache in my chest spread throughout the rest of my torso. Tears filled my eyes.

"I do. I just need some time to process all of this."

Ron was gracious. "I understand. Take my card and this book. I think it might shed some light on your specific situation. Call me anytime."

I nodded my head and took his card and the book titled, *A Guidebook to Breaking the Generational Curse*. I blinked away tears and looked at Ron. A moment of recognition passed between us. He smiled and handed me a black plastic bag with another book inside.

"Put that book and my card in the bag, and don't let anyone else see it."

I put the card inside the book and put the book in the bag. I nodded my head. "Thank you," was all I could manage to say.

Ron smiled again. "You're welcome. Now make sure to have a look at everything I gave you, and don't forget to call me if you need someone to talk to."

He got up from his seat and walked the few steps to the stage to start the process of packing up his stuff. I held the bag tight and walked the short distance to the door.

● ● ●

As I emerged from the room into the convention center my senses were saturated by the massive crowd. The freaks were out in the middle of the day, no longer satisfied to own just the night. Anxiety reared its ugly head, and I struggled to maintain composure, traveling against the flow of traffic to reach the doors that led outside. I almost broke into a run on the sidewalk as I worked my way back to the rental car.

Once inside the car, I shut and locked the door, then broke down. Tears of fear and of mourning ran down my face. Wiping them away was pointless, as they just kept coming. I sat in the car for a long time before I shifted into drive and went back to the hotel. I vowed to never return to Roswell during the UFO festival, no matter what drew me there.

● ● ●

It wasn't until the flight home that I looked at the contents of the black plastic bag Ron Lincoln gave me. The book on generational curses was in there, along with another. I pulled it out of the bag to get a better look. It was a bible for new Christians. I regarded it for a moment before stuffing it back inside the bag.

I frowned as I thought about my religious beliefs. I believed in a god, but did not have any concrete ideas about what that meant. I set the bag aside, closed my eyes, and slept the rest of the way home.

THE END OF ALL THINGS

• 18 •

I tried to get my life back to a state of normal once I came home from my trip. Work was monotonous and dull. Being home was even more empty and depressing than before. I left the bag with Ron Lincoln's book, card, and the bible on the kitchen table for several days. The compulsion to pick them up and start reading was strong, but I resisted. My fear continued to be driven by the concept that knowledge, once absorbed, was impossible to unlearn.

One night, while making a box of cheap macaroni and cheese, my eyes kept wandering to that stupid black bag. It was tempting to throw it away, but that would do no good. I'd just dig it out of the trash and set it right back on the table. There was only one way to resolve this problem.

I scooped some macaroni and cheese into a bowl and sat down at the table. With a mouthful of pasta and a cheese-like sauce, I fished Ron Lincoln's book, *A Guidebook to Breaking the Generational Curse*, out of the bag.

Time slipped away, and I read the whole thing in one sitting. Granted, it wasn't a very thick book, but still it was quite an accomplishment. His words spoke to me in a way I could never have imagined, and I was convinced me that I was the object of a generational curse. The isolation of the people described in that book was so similar to the members of my own family, along with our separation from society, whether intentional or subtly influenced by unseen forces. A shudder ran through me.

Charlie whimpered at my side and circled by the sliding glass door. I got up from the table and opened it to let him out. A summer breeze wafted in from outside. As the smells of pine and dirt filled my nostrils I stepped into the backyard. It took a moment for my eyes to adjust to the darkness of night. A sudden chill caused an involuntary shiver as I scanned the dark, overgrown field. A rustle in the undergrowth where the field met the forest caused my heart to skip.

Something moved way out in the distance. It could have been any number of things, but it wasn't any number of things. It was one specific thing. A diminutive creature with a big head and long arms appeared in silhouette just on the edge of my property. I felt paralyzed by fear. It had been so long since I'd seen anything unusual that I wondered if it was my imagination creating shapes in the darkness. And then the sneaking grey beast stepped forward and raised a long-fingered hand to its lipless mouth.

I found my voice. "Charlie, come inside. Let's go, boy."

He came bounding around the corner and ran behind me into the house. I walked backwards never taking my eyes off the little monster as it moved slow and deliberate toward me. Fear spread like cancer through my cells as adrenaline rushed through my veins. Breathing became difficult.

Once inside, I closed the door, locked it, and flipped off the light over the kitchen table. With my face close to the door I stared into the field. Breath fogged the glass. I wiped it away and searched in the distance. The creature was nowhere to be seen. I closed the blinds so fast they swayed back and forth so hard I thought they might fly off their rails. My breath came in quick bursts and thoughts swirled in my head so fast I was sure to pass out.

Without thinking, I grabbed the black bag off the table and retreated to the living room. With a shaking hand, I picked up the remote and turned on the television. The news droned on and did nothing to grant me even a moment of comfort. Charlie launched himself onto the sofa next to me and laid down. I closed my eyes and struggled to slow my respiration and my thoughts.

A while later I dumped the remaining contents of the bag onto the coffee table. Ron Lincoln's business card fell out along with the bible. I picked up the book and turned it over, admiring the faux leather. There was a faint memory of cracking open our family bible at one time. The only thing I remembered reading was the first line of Genesis. After my mother died the book disappeared. I assumed my old man either tossed it or packed it away in some corner of the house where no one could ever find it.

As I opened this bible to the first page, a small piece of paper fell out. On it, Ron Lincoln had written instructions. *Start with John, then call me.*

It took some time to find the book of John, but I did and read it in one sitting. I learned all about Jesus; his life, his death, and his plan to save the world. It seemed even crazier than being abducted by aliens. I closed the Bible and set it on the coffee table next to Ron Lincoln's note. My phone was on the kitchen table and it was tempting to grab it and call him, but I didn't.

● ● ●

The next night at work Alicia arrived early. I'd promised to tell her all about the trip and had successfully avoided her for over a week after putting her off when I picked up Charlie. Relaying the tale meant telling her the entire truth about what had happened to me. The mental block I felt before was gone, but repeating my experience was something I wished I never had to do again.

On the first perimeter check of her shift, we walked slow. Our coworker John was late as usual, and I was in no hurry to go home. I took my time laying it all out for her. Her eyes gleamed and she grinned like the Cheshire Cat at the mention of the bright lights and the presence of the greys. As I continued to explain the abduction, experimentation and the aftermath, her mood was more contemplative and less jovial. By the time I got to the point where she showed up at my door, she was speechless.

We were silent by the time we returned to the guard shack. Alicia plopped down into a chair and looked at me for the first time since I had started talking. I feared her pity but thought the compassion I saw in her eyes was worse. It meant that she cared about what happened to me.

Fighting back tears, she spoke. "I don't even know what to say. That sounds horrible. I mean I've heard accounts of alien abduction, but they all seemed so distant. What you've been through, Alex, I can't even imagine"

I smiled. "That's not the strangest part."

Her eyes went wide. "I don't think I can bear anymore."

My laugh alleviated some of her tension. I sat down in a chair of my own and swiveled to face her. "I went to Roswell looking for answers. The funny thing is, I came back with more questions. Aside from my trip to The Bottomless Lakes State Park, it was mostly a terrible experience. None of that was your fault. I can't thank you enough for planning everything out for me."

Alicia smirked and leaned forward. "What did you find out?"

I rolled my neck to work out a kink on the right side. "Ron Lincoln thinks that the aliens are not aliens at all, but demons creating vivid hallucinations, and I am in danger of demonic oppression or possession."

Now, her mouth dropped open. "Are you serious? How can he know that?"

"I don't remember all the specifics, just that he believes they are using our vision of an interstellar future to trick us, and that abductions are a form of torture for their enjoyment. Oh, and it's likely part of a generational curse."

"Did he have any suggestions about how to stop it?"

I paused, wondering if I should tell her. At that point, there was really nothing left to lose. "Yes. He said they only respond to the name of Jesus."

Alicia spun around in the chair, a big smile spread

across her face. "Is he for real? The name of Jesus. Did you try it?"

"No, I haven't tried it. I'm still working it all out in my mind. I think I should go see Carla and see what she knows about all this."

"You absolutely have to talk to her. There is no doubt in my mind she's heard of this before."

I agreed and started thinking about how to approach the situation. Carla was sensitive about the name Ron Lincoln, and she must have known about his theories. Both of them had studied UFOs and aliens for years and came to different conclusions. I needed to know what she thought about this Jesus idea before deciding if that was the best route to take. A familiar sinking feeling formed in my stomach as I thought about the confrontation that was sure to come.

● ● ●

The night before I saw Carla I dreamed that I was my grandfather, naked and growling out in the backyard. My family had locked themselves inside the house and I could hear sirens in the distant corners of my mind. My thoughts were not my own, replaced by something instinctual, something animal. And like an animal, I was led by an insatiable hunger for destruction.

When the police arrived and attempted to reason with me I fought them off with a strength that was not my own. The power was both superhuman and subhuman, intelligent and malevolent at the same time.

224

It took four men to finally take me down. I inhaled and ate dirt as one of them pressed his knee into my back and two of them cuffed me.

When I woke up from the dream I was more confused than ever. Much of the situation with my grandfather was a mystery to me. In the dream, I experienced my grandfather's thoughts as he realized the thing controlling him wanted to stop him from getting closer to the truth. It was a last ditch effort to destroy his life. And it looked like it had won.

● ● ●

On the way to Carla's house, I rehearsed what I would say. I trusted her with the information, but there was no way I could speak to her in a direct manner about the growing connection I suspected between me and my grandfather. And I couldn't make the slightest mention of Ron Lincoln without her melting down. I wondered if I was being naïve to trust her with any of this information, but based on her past actions, she intended nothing but good for me. I had no reason to think otherwise.

It was late morning by the time I arrived in downtown Avondale. The clouds crowded out any patches of blue sky. The weather forecast had threatened rain for several days, but it had yet to come. It seemed the storm was in a holding pattern until conditions were perfect.

If my surprise visit was to remain a surprise, I needed to be a little sneaky. I parked the truck a street over, well out of view.

A droplet of water landed on my arm as I started my short walk to Carla's house. Another landed on my nose. The promised rain had arrived, and I quickened my pace. By the time I reached the front door, a steady shower poured from the heavens. I rang the doorbell and stood back, waiting for my host. I felt calm, which was not what I expected considering the circumstances of my visit. I rang the doorbell again after a few seconds passed with no answer.

A waft of warm air scented with fresh bread and chocolate chip cookies rushed out as the door swung open. The smell was intoxicating and stripped me of my defenses. I thought I may have detected hints of that one of a kind coffee.

Carla stood in the doorway, looking perplexed. She wiped her hands on her white apron. "Alex, why this is a surprise. What brings you out here?"

Shedding my plan to be somewhat deceitful and smooth in obtaining information from her, I spit out the primary intention for my visit. "I need to know all the information you have about my grandfather. I am positive that what is happening to me may be the same thing that happened to him all those years ago. And you are the only one I can turn to for answers."

She hesitated for a moment as if considering her options. It was nothing more than a small glint in her eye that betrayed nothing, but there was subtle tell that slipped right past me in the moment.

"I know we discussed the possibility of a connection," she said absently.

"Well, come on in. Let's get you out of this rain and have a little talk. Just go into the parlor and I'll be right in." She motioned me inside before turning and walking toward the kitchen to grab some refreshments.

Nothing much had changed. The furniture and overall decorative chaos of the room remained the same. Notebooks were scattered on the table. A couple of worn looking hardcover books were left open. I sat down in the brown armchair to wait for Carla. That was when I saw my name scrawled across the top of a page in one of the open notebooks.

The air was sucked out of the room as a seed of panic crept into my chest. My face felt hot. I raised my head above the back of the chair and looked over my shoulder. Carla was nowhere in sight. The open notebook with my name written on it called to me. I leaned forward to see if anything else stood out. There were words on the page, but nothing specific I could make out without getting closer. The pit in my stomach told me something was not right.

I jumped when Carla appeared in the room. I hadn't heard her coming and wondered if she saw me snooping. She smiled and set down a tray with two cups of coffee and a plate of those delicious cookies. My mouth watered. I returned the smile and hoped she didn't notice the tension in my shoulders. As she sat down her eyes remained fixed on me, questioning my intentions.

She appeared almost relaxed when I saw her eyes widen as she noticed the open notebook with my name written on the page. To redirect my attention, she moved her gaze from the coffee table to me and crossed her arms. "Now tell me, what can I do for you?"

I leaned forward, hoping my voice did not waver. "I need to know if there is anything else I should know about my grandfather. Was he the first person in my family to have experienced alien abduction or supernatural activity?"

Carla looked thoughtful for a moment, planning her response with the greatest of care. "As far as I know he was the first and only member of your family to be abducted. He did talk a bit about his sister, who dabbled in the occult with a bit of white magic. She was ostracized from the family after they discovered her secret and was forced to live a life apart from them. At least that's his story."

I was shocked by the revelation. "I never heard of her. What was her name?"

She looked up as though searching invisible files in the air in front of her face. "Let's see. I think it was Francine or something like that. Why? Is that important to you?"

There was something she wasn't telling me. "No. I was just wondering about the possible generational connection between what is happening now and what happened then."

Carla shrugged and looked away. "I really wish I had more information to give to you, but that's all I know."

She was lying and doing a good job of it. What was she hiding?

I took a chance to throw her off her game and rattle her cage a little bit. "Is it true that the name of Jesus can stop the aliens from abducting someone?"

Her eyes flashed and she froze. I'd struck a nerve and kept my eyes focused on her, daring her to lie again.

"I've heard theories from crackpots and amateurs. Have you tried it?"

"No. I was just curious what, if anything, you knew about it."

Her short, closed answers told me I'd get nowhere. She had no interest in diving into the depths of my thoughts or experiences like she had in the past. The silence became awkward as I looked at her, expecting some sort of encouragement or advice. She leaned forward and clasped her hands in front of her, but said nothing.

I broke first. "Thank you for your time, Carla. I'm sorry for interrupting your day."

"Oh, it is no bother at all. Feel free to drop in anytime." She stood and stole an almost imperceptible glance at the notebook.

I got up and followed her into the foyer. The pit in my stomach refused to let me leave without that notebook. I impressed myself by coming up with a tiny lie on the spot that was brilliant when compared to my failed attempt to deceive her earlier.

"Carla, I left my phone on the coffee table." I had, in fact, never taken it out of my pocket.

She paused for a half second, as though considering denying my simple request. "Ok. Go on and get it. I have some baking to get to. You know the way out."

The two of us walked in opposite directions, Carla to the kitchen, and me into the parlor. The notebook still lay open, calling to me. I reached down, grabbed it, and stuffed it under my t-shirt before there was any time to think about what I was doing. The flat impression created by the notebook was rather obvious, but I hoped it would go unnoticed since she had decided to stop playing the gracious hostess and not see me to the door.

I tried to remain calm as I strolled toward the door, doing my best to hide the notebook. The blood rushed through my ears and I felt light-headed. The notebook wasn't my property, but it was clear there was something in it I needed to see. Carla had been evasive and anxious to be rid of me. The theft was easy to justify.

I opened the door and walked out onto the front porch. "Thank you again, Carla. I hope you have a good day."

"You too, Alex."

I let out a big breath after closing the door behind me, and half-ran, half-walked back to my truck. It wouldn't be long before Carla noticed the notebook missing. I wondered if she would dare ask for it, especially once I found out what she was hiding from me.

• 19 •

I drove to a nearby park with the notebook on the seat next to me. There was no way I could wait until I got home to read its contents. It was no surprise that Carla kept notes on the people who came to her little Avondale Paranormal Society meetings. Her life's work was spent researching and learning as much as she could about UFOs and aliens. Had she never even considered the possibility that they could be demons?

I found a parking spot on the backside of the park, next to an empty play structure. No kids were out during the storm. The rain spattered on the roof and hood, punctuated by the occasional distant rumble of thunder. I picked up the notebook and turned to the first page. My name was written across it, along with my date of birth, home address, occupation, and living situation.

The next few pages were dedicated to the recounting of my story up to the point when I met Carla. There was nothing in it that I hadn't expected, but I had to wonder if the audio of the Avondale Paranormal

Society meetings were secretly recorded. There was no way she could have remembered everything she wrote down on those pages.

It was clear she had considered the possible connection between me and my grandfather with a two-word question that was bolded and circled. *Generational Curse?*

The breath left my body. Carla had lied to me by omission. Whenever the sightings and abduction were mentioned, she always spoke of it as a positive experience, a testament to the special attention paid to my family line. If that were true why had she referred to it as a potential curse?

I flipped the page and continued reading about a member of my family I'd never heard of before that day, my Great Aunt Francine.

Francine was an oddity. She was sickly as a child, and therefore perceived as a burden. Her brother was adored, and this made her very jealous.

She became interested in witchcraft as an escape from her life. She was fascinated by the idea that a person could influence those around her and therefore acquire a form of power over them. Until she was shunned by her family she kept her practices a secret.

As with most people, she started small and gradually became more and more involved with the practice of witchcraft. Her rituals and spells grew more powerful and she gained the attention of several prominent spiritual entities.

I stopped reading. How could Carla possibly have known this information? Either she found out through interviewing my grandfather or she had met with Francine in person. It was further confirmation of her willful deception of me, and fury welled up in my chest, replacing the fear.

After she was discovered, Francine cursed her family throughout all remaining generations with the help of her spirit guides. She vowed to have them tormented into insanity, until the last of the bloodline was wiped out.

Ron Lincoln's theory and my own half-baked assumptions were confirmed. The supernatural experiences that plagued me were part of a generational curse. I felt vindicated. The doubts I had about my own intuition evaporated. I was foolish for doubting myself or Ron Lincoln. It was clear that Carla played a bigger role than I realized, but the extent of her involvement remained to be seen. Had she intended that I would find her notes, and if so, to what end?

I still held the notebook in front of me, but my thoughts were far away. I was the last of the bloodline that Francine hoped to wipe out. I wondered if this curse had anything to do with my solitary lifestyle. It must, even though I assumed for so long that I lived the way I did by choice or circumstance. It was hard to grasp the concept that there was a supernatural plot against me.

There was no doubt of my experience with supernatural entities, but could they really be the result of a curse placed on my family by my great aunt from so long ago? If it was true, I already knew how to break its power by reading Ron's book and the bible.

I set the notebook down. Stealing Carla's notes had been necessary, but also served as a catalyst for setting a chain of events into motion that could not be stopped. I needed to arm myself with the truth, and if I truly believed what Ron Lincoln taught, there was no time to waste.

Then again, if these creatures were really from another planet, abducting humans and performing experiments, Ron's methods would prove ineffective. I wasn't sure which was worse; the unknown consequences of taking his advice, or trying to break the curse and it having no effect at all.

I closed the notebook and set it on the seat next to me. The rain slowed and I started my truck, shifted into gear, and began to drive home. Thoughts crowded my brain and it was a struggle to stay focused on the road ahead of me. I needed to talk to someone who could help me. Someone who I knew would understand.

Shelby's Restaurant was just ahead. There were still a couple of hours before it would be dark, but the lighted sign was visible under the cloudy sky. The 's' at the end of the name was missing, so it read 'elb', instead of 'elb's' as it had when Carla and I met there months ago. When I said it out loud it sounded a lot like help. I pulled into the dirt lot and parked far away from the building. It was time to call Ron Lincoln.

There was a moment of panic as I struggled to remember where I put his business card. I pulled my wallet out of my pocket and searched for it, hoping the memory of grabbing it off the coffee table in my living room before the visit to Carla was true. I sighed with relief when I found it. I snatched the plain card with Ron's name and phone number on the front and his personal note on the back out of my wallet.

My hand trembled as I dialed the number. Not out of fear, but of expectation or perhaps the knowledge that something was about to change. He answered on the second ring.

"Hello, this is Ron."

I had trouble remembering my own name and

was silent.

"Hello. Is anyone there?"

"Yes," I answered, finding my bearings. "You probably don't remember me, but my name is Alex Mayfield and I saw you in Roswell. I was the only one who stayed until the end of your presentation."

"Of course I remember you, Alex. I've been thinking about you quite a bit since we last saw each other."

The fact that he remembered me was not a surprise, but the idea that he was still thinking about me well past our meeting struck me as odd.

"You have?"

"Yes. There have been many times I've been impressed to pray for you. Is everything okay?"

Is everything okay? Of course, everything was not okay. How could anything be okay?

"No. Things are crap right now. I'm sorry to be so blunt, but there's no other way to put it."

There was brief silence on the other end of the conversation.

"Why don't you tell me about it and we can figure it out together."

I burst into tears. His words were what I had hoped Carla would have said to me, but she treated me with indifference. The gravity of the trouble I faced pulled me toward despair. I had nowhere to turn, and no one to fight on my behalf.

Ron was silent while I fumbled through a retelling of my visit with Carla and the new information I learned about my family. The realization that my solitary existence was not a choice, but the result of a sibling's grudge two generations removed hit me at that moment and I cried out, desperate for someone to help me find a way out of this mess.

"Alex, I can help you, but you have to trust me. Can you do that?"

I had no reason not to trust him.

"Yes."

"If you want to be rid of this curse for good you are going to have to make a decision about whether or not to follow Jesus. And you can't fake that decision. It has to be real or else there will be no conversion and you will have no power over this thing."

I longed to be rid of the curse, but fear of the unknown prevented me from taking any action. Why was it so hard for me to set aside my fear and the illusion of control over my own life?

"I want to. I really do. It's just so hard to let go. That sounds stupid, I know, but it's true."

"Alex, it's not stupid. Jesus says to come to him as a little child with full trust and faith. It's hard for adults to break through the mental barriers we set up for ourselves that protect us from perceived harm."

An ache spread from my chest. I knew his words were true, and that there was no malice in what he said, but years of building walls to keep everyone out were hard to break down. I felt the presence of something beyond my senses that waited for me to reach out and grab it.

"I don't know if I can." It was all I could say.

"No one can force you to make that decision, Alex. It has to be you."

I longed to take that truth inside and push out all the lies that bound me to my familial fate. The ache in my chest spread; a desire to experience the truth for what might have been the first time in my life. I needed to break free from isolation, escape the death my life had become and embrace life.

"I'm ready."

Ron asked me to recite a simple prayer and make it my own. I admitted that I was lost and in need of a savior. I confessed and asked for forgiveness of my sins, and repented of my old life. I asked Jesus to be Lord of my life and to live inside of me.

At that moment, a strange sensation came over me. The ache in my heart was replaced by a warmth that radiated from the center of my chest to the tips of my fingers and toes. The fear that controlled me was temporarily replaced by a joy that caused me to burst into fresh tears. Years of guilt and hidden shame were lifted from me. I blinked tears away and felt as if I could truly see for the first time in my life. And then Ron told me something that struck terror into my heart.

"Alex, you must be warned that the demons attacking you will come back for one last battle in an attempt to steal back your soul. Of everything you have faced so far, this will be the worst. You need to be prepared to fight. These entities have had centuries of experience and are well versed in treachery."

My eyes grew wide and a transfusion of fear rushed through my veins, threatening to steal away my moment of peace. I wasn't ready to face the terror that I knew in my heart was coming.

"I wish I could be with you in person, but I cannot. But don't worry. You have all you need to deal with the spiritual battle. And I will cover you in prayer and ask my connections to do the same. I just ask that you stay brave, alert, and dive into the Word. Also, tell no one of my involvement in this. If I hope to have any impact at all on this alien invasion I need to stay irrelevant. Do you understand?"

I nodded my head, then realized he couldn't see me on the other side of the phone.

"Yes."

I thanked Ron in ways that seemed insufficient. When my words ran dry I was wrecked with exhaustion. The drive home was automatic and it was surprising I made it in one piece since I remembered none of it.

Charlie was as excited as ever to see me. I walked past him in a fog and crashed on the couch. I was out the second my head hit the cushion. There were no dreams that night.

• 20 •

ummer faded into autumn. The first leaves of fall transformed into the brightest version of themselves before releasing their grip on life and floating to the ground to be recycled as food for the next generation. I had yet to have my promised final confrontation. Carla's notebook sat on my coffee table, a constant reminder of my fate.

I did everything I could to distract myself from facing the challenge. I continued my work as a security guard at Avondale Farms. At home, I restained the front porch and refreshed the paint on the exterior of the house. I even dragged the tractor out of the barn and turned the overgrown fields into bales of hay to give to the neighbors with horses and livestock.

And even with all that distraction, I had sleepless nights plagued by nightmarish visions of little grey men with the darkest of eyes that reached into the depths of my spirit, hungry to devour the very essence of my being, my worn and tired soul. I did everything I could to bury my fear, but my subconscious refused to allow me peace.

During that time, I read through the entirety of the bible and learned a great deal about the history of Christianity and the nature of God. I had always assumed He was a sort of eye in the sky master, overlooking his creation, but not really involved in the day to day operation. But actually diving into the text of the Bible, God repeatedly revealed himself as a personal Lord who delighted in rescuing His children from the clutches of eternal death, in spite of overwhelming odds. I thought I should find comfort in that promise, but I only felt anxiety and fear.

There was also the matter of Carla herself. I had not seen or heard from her since I'd stolen the notebook. She never contacted me, and I made no attempt to attend any of the Avondale Paranormal Society meetings. Somehow I needed to know her role in all of this. She presented herself as a sort of benevolent guide and friend, but I suspected that her loyalties lay somewhere else.

● ● ●

All of that contemplation and lack of action was maddening. That's how I ended up dressed in all black, standing in Carla's backyard, peering through the windows. It was cold and wet from the constant drizzle of that October night, but I ignored my discomfort. I sought the truth about Carla and this was the only way I knew how to get it. I had to spy on her.

Nothing happened for the longest time. The lights

were on inside, and it was obvious that Carla was hosting some sort of dinner party with Phil and Ellie – the time reversing couple that had attended meetings of the Avondale Paranormal Society with me – and another man I had never seen. He was tall, thin, and pale with a shaved head. His eyes were set far back into his skull, casting a shadow over them, so much so that I could not see their color. I shivered at the sight of him.

After dinner and a few pleasantries, the four of them moved into the study that was just off the parlor. I stood in the shadows of the trees, hiding from view. I wished that I could have heard the conversation, but I was too far away.

To my surprise, the lights in the room switched off after they had all entered. A prickle of apprehension ran up my back; another devil dancing on my grave. I had to move closer to see what was going on in there.

One small light and then another broke through the total darkness of the room as I crept closer to the window. I could just make out the shape of someone lighting candles. The low light of the small flames cast shifting shadows in the room. Carla's back was to the window and I had to move to the side to get a better view.

Carla, Phil, Ellie, and the mystery man formed a circle, bowed their heads, and held hands. There were about a dozen squares of glossy paper laid out on the oak surface of the coffee table surrounded by candles of various heights. The sound of a collective hum filtered through the pane of glass. From my vantage point, I could not make out what was on those pieces of paper. I needed to get higher.

I walked a short distance to the shed in the backyard and found it unlocked. My eyes adjusted to the gloom inside and in the ambient light I made out a wooden step ladder. As quiet as possible I carried the ladder to the window. Afraid that opening it fully would cause the metal brackets to squeak I set it against the side of the house without making a sound. I climbed the steps in slow motion. Still hidden in darkness, I almost threw myself off the ladder once I reached the top and saw what was laid out on the table. The dozen or so squares of paper were pictures of people. Most I did not recognize. But one of those pictures was mine.

Clinging to the ladder and looking at my picture on that table, I felt exposed to more than just the elements of the night. Whatever ritual that strange crew was performing in there was a part of what was happening to me. Maybe a big part. Carla was clearly not who she pretended to be. Her sympathetic mask hid a monstrous heart.

The candles in the room began to flicker as though pushed by a breeze, even though the windows were closed tight. The four people inside the house lifted their heads until they were looking straight up at the ceiling. Carla's wild head of hair moved with the wind that swirled around the room.

Some of the candles blew out. Others held on, shining with what light they had. Carla, Phil, Ellie, and the mystery man opened their eyes as one. I almost screamed at the sight of them. All the color in their eyes was replaced by pools of darkness, similar to the greys. I took one hand and covered my mouth, shivered, and allowed tears of fear to fall down my face.

What happened next chilled my blood. From the shadows of the room, four creatures emerged, birthed from the darkness. Four creatures I recognized from my experiences and recurring nightmares. The Greys. Each possessed the same oversized head with gigantic black eyes and the small amorphous body. They walked toward their human hosts as one, united in their purpose.

I pressed myself into the ladder as fear coursed through my body. I needed to leave, but I was frozen in place. One of the greys on the far side of the room turned toward me, and I felt its piercing gaze burn into my soul. It was impossible for it to know I was there outside the window, but I was certain that it must. The remaining candles in the room extinguished themselves as one, and I couldn't see past my own faint reflection.

I jumped off the side of the ladder, dropped to the ground, and hugged myself flat against the outside wall of the house. No one, not even the monsters inside, should have been able to see me through the solid wall. In an attempt to avoid further detection, I crawled on the ground toward the corner of the house, out of view of the back windows. Once there, I sprang to my feet and took off running into a neighbors yard.

My lungs felt like they were on the verge of collapse after the three block sprint to my truck. Breathing heavy, I ripped open the door and fought every urge within me to just peel out on the street. I steadied myself and started the truck with shaking hands. Instead of racing down the road, I kept the lights off and drove slow until I reached the main drag. Only then did I put the pedal to the metal and screeched away from downtown Avondale.

On the drive home, my brain was on fire. It was clear to me that something evil was taking place at Carla's home. The only picture on the table that I recognized was mine. Still, I felt in my gut that each one of those people were going through a similar experience. There was no doubt in my mind that what happened to me was not the work of benign life forms from another galaxy, but demons bent on destroying me in any way they could.

●　●　●

That night I slept in fits and starts, as had become the norm for me. During one of my bouts of unconsciousness, I was woken up by the sound of Charlie's claws tapping against the hardwood floor, and a soft whimper he usually reserved for the strongest of thunderstorms. I opened my eyes to total darkness. All ambient light was gone.

After a few seconds, I was able to make out shapes in the room. At the far end of the sofa, two forms materialized from the ether. They were quickly followed by identical forms on each side of me, and I felt a presence behind my head, but refused to turn around. Their bulbous heads, small bodies, and gigantic eyes made it obvious that they were greys. They stood still and stared at me with scrutinizing eyes. I tried to move, but couldn't. I opened my mouth to speak and nothing came out. I wanted to scream, but my body refused to comply with my demands. Charlie started to scratch at the front door.

The grey to my right leaned forward and peered into eyes, just inches from my face. And while it had no expression, I had the sense it felt joy at my discomfort. I sank deeper into the couch cushions, willing myself to disappear into it. If this was the final fight for my soul, I was nowhere near ready.

I closed my eyes to prepare for the worst. What

that was, I wasn't sure. They'd already abducted me, tortured me, scoured my soul, and left me a shell of the person I'd been, but I was certain that demons had all kinds of ways to destroy a human.

After a few seconds of anticipation, I opened my eyes. The greys were gone as if they had never been there at all. I reached over and felt for Charlie, who was asleep by my side on the floor. A tremble started in my hand and spread to the rest of my body. I knew I had been visited by my very own dark angels, and their visit was a warning. They knew I was at Carla's house that night. And the message was clear. They were coming to punish me for my sins.

I lay awake the rest of the night, confined to my living room, watching through the front window as the darkness of night gave way to the soft light of dawn. I prayed to God like never before, desperate for rescue. Crying, I surrendered my life to Him, knowing deep inside that He was the only one who could save me from these monsters and break the curse on my family.

Once the sun had fully risen, I slept from morning into early afternoon. It was the best sleep I'd had in months. I awoke refreshed and felt alive. All of my dark thoughts were temporarily forgotten while I reveled in clarity. My brain allowed me to enjoy a moment in the light, a reprieve from the zombie-like fog that had become my routine.

That flash of joy was brief, but it allowed me to hope again, to dream of a future not ruled by fear. I caught a glimpse of the person I could be and longed to be that way all the time. That short moment of positive reflection was the push I needed to make myself brave enough to face my darkest fears, and conquer the demons haunting me.

• 21 •

A week passed with no word from Carla, and no surprise visits from the greys. Despite this, I knew by intuition or supernatural revelation that both were preparing to come for me and time was short. The beasts who tormented me longed to devour my soul and would not be so quick to give up just because I'd found religion. The day was coming when I would have to stand up to my greatest enemy. Despite my newfound faith and renewed energy, I was still afraid.

The feeling that something big was brewing beyond the natural veil of this world refused to leave me. At that time, I studied the book of Revelation more in-depth, struggling to comprehend the beginning of the end of the world. I did not have much interest in the endless debate about the reality of a rapture of the church prior to the tribulation. Still, the thought that aliens may be offered as an explanation and a way to convince people to accept other end times events intrigued me to no end.

It made perfect sense to use aliens to explain the

mass disappearance of a large chunk of the population, paving the road for a world leader to step up and take control of a world in chaos. Then again, it could also be a leader from the 'alien' race that could raise themselves up as savior using a human vessel as a meat puppet. Either way, thinking about the implications of that future was not comforting.

But that was a concern for another day. I had other things to worry about. I was near the end of my self-paced spiritual training, and the time was coming when I could no longer cower from my demons, but would have to confront and defeat them with a crushing death blow.

My mind spun in circles creating multiple fatalistic scenarios. Every thought ended badly. At some point, the continuous speculation became too exhausting. I lost the will and energy to consider all of the possible outcomes and focused on the only one that mattered. Evil would end its reign of terror in me.

● ● ●

The night sky was crystal clear. I sat on the porch with Charlie in my flannel lined jeans and a heavy wool sweater. The air was cool and unexpectedly dry for that time of year. I felt a sense of satisfaction and peace that was hard to explain. A cloud of dread still hung over my head, but I managed to find joy in the simple things, like that moment in time.

Since surrendering my will to God's will, I had

not seen any sign of the greys. Even my dreams were no longer dominated by nightmarish visions. I wondered if those wretched creatures were waiting until I felt a false sense of security before striking. The Holy Spirit kept me spiritually motivated to remain vigilant, feeding myself on the Word of God as often as I could.

All of that studying and meditating spilled over into the rest of my life. At work, I became known as the resident 'bible thumper'. But not because I came in bragging and boasting about how perfect and godly I was. I brought my Bible, notebook, and other reading material in with me, and my co-workers noticed. Alicia was the first to call me by my new nickname, but it was never uttered in a negative context. With a little more time, I might get her to come around to my new way of living.

I went back inside and let Charlie go to the bathroom while I locked up the rest of the house, changed into a t-shirt and gym shorts, used the restroom myself, and brushed my teeth. When enough time had passed, I walked downstairs and let Charlie back in from the other side of the house.

As I closed the sliding glass door that led into the backyard, I thought I saw a shadow pass across the overgrown field in the distance. I admit that my senses were heightened, always expecting a confrontation that had yet to come, and therefore prone to seeing things that weren't really there. It could have just as easily been a cloud blotting out the light of the moon in that specific section of the property. I stared through the glass into the backyard, searching and seeing nothing.

Charlie and I went upstairs. I had moved from the living room to the bedroom. It was all a part of my new existence. I made a promise to myself to let go of fear and live life. The first few nights were hard, but I managed to fall into a routine, and before I knew it I slept as sound as I had before the close encounters started.

Several minutes later, sleep stole my last vestiges of consciousness. Just as I sunk into a dream, a blinding light filled the room. I snapped open my eyes. It was the same bright light as the night I was taken. Instead of succumbing to the paralysis of fear, I sucked in a deep breath and jumped out of bed. Charlie bounded to my side and started to growl. His bravado faded as the familiar hum rumbled and grew louder. He whimpered and crawled under the bed when the light began to pulsate. Instinct told me to bolt for the door, and I was halfway to the threshold when a harsh gasp escaped my lips.

In each of the four corners of the room stood a grey. They were as hideous and hateful as I remembered with their huge heads, soulless eyes, and long spindle-like fingers. They all stared at me, their eyes windows into the abyss beyond the grave. I swallowed hard. My eyes darted around the room looking for any sign of movement toward me. They just stood there, watching me.

Sensing an opportunity I might not have later, I tore open the door and dashed into the hall. At the landing, I looked down the stairs and saw one of the greys guarding the bottom of the steps.

To the left of me, another grey blocked access to the remaining rooms on the second floor. My heart beat hard, and I fought to maintain control. Now was not the time to panic.

Ignoring the instinct to cower and beg for mercy, I walked down the steps with purpose. The grey at the bottom of the stairs held its position. Its eyes bore into mine, daring me to come closer. Five steps from the bottom I stopped and opened my mouth to speak.

"In the name of Jesus, son of God, I command you to leave." My voice was shaky and filled with false courage.

The grey's expression changed into one of confusion before it vanished in a puff of black smoke. The smell of sulfur replaced its presence. I wondered what happened to it at that moment. Was it banished to hell, or simply removed from my sight? Either option was fine with me as long as it was out of my way.

There were two more of the grey beasts downstairs. One blocked my access to the front door, and another the way into the kitchen. I stormed up to the little monster at the front door and repeated my command with more confidence. Its dark eyes glimmered with shock before dissipating into a cloud of smoke. I smiled to myself. *This was too easy.*

When I opened the front door, there were hundreds if not thousands of those short big-headed demons as far as I could see. They turned toward me as one, silent sentries for their invisible master, the devil. My courage failed for a moment and I took a step back, my knees weak. I uttered a short prayer for help, forced myself to walk forward, and grabbed onto the front porch railing at the top of the stairs. The cold wind bit right through my thin t-shirt and nylon athletic shorts.

I held onto the railing and stepped into the yard. A frenzy of lights in all colors flashed around me. I looked up at the sky. It was filled with an endless number of spinning disc-shaped UFOs. White, pink, green, and orange lights spun with fury. The gravity of the fight ahead of me was overwhelming. A familiar tremble started in my hand and moved to the rest of my body.

It's nothing more than an illusion, Alex.

The thought came into my brain like a gentle

wave that felt true, though I doubted the words. A horde of demons surrounded me, and the odds were impossible. How could I ever hope to stand against an enemy that was infinite?

You are not alone, Alex. I am with you.

I leaned against the post at the bottom of the steps and closed my eyes. I didn't want this. I never asked for it. And yet there I was.

I slipped to my knees, held my hands up to the sky and sang praises to my God. At first, I felt nothing and waited for despair to overtake me, as the demons prepared to attack me. My song continued and soon my fingertips began to tingle with a warmth that spread through my hands, down my arms, and into the rest of my body.

While the feeling invaded every part of my being, I opened my eyes and stood up with my hands still extended toward heaven. The countless number of greys and UFOs focused their attention on me but did not advance. I took several steps into the yard and they moved aside, clearing a path for me. These monsters that tormented me before kept their distance. That should have given me some measure of comfort, but it only increased my anxiety. What if I was unable to live up to the challenge of a formidable enemy? I closed my eyes and cried out to God to rescue me.

In that instant, I felt an explosion of power radiate from my body in all directions. I cracked my eyelids and saw that the hideous creatures had moved farther away from me. I was enclosed on all sides by a horde of greys in a radius of a hundred feet or more. I took another step forward and the protective circle moved with me. It reminded me of the supernatural protection that Meshach, Shadrach, and Abednego

252

experienced in the fiery furnace.

I kept moving forward until I reached the middle of the front yard. The lights of the flying discs above me dazzled the sky in crazy patterns. The combined power of their propulsion created a wind storm that set off the wind chime under the front porch. My hair whipped around my head. If this was an illusion or a special effect, it was the best I had ever seen.

Evil boxed me in on every side. Yet with the power of the Holy Spirit, I was able to stand against it. I cried out to God, thanking him for his intervention.

To get a better idea of the odds, I spun around. Alien creatures filled the fields up to and beyond the line of trees at the back of the property. As I assessed the size of the enemy, a beam of light brighter than all the others broke through the barrier of shining metal discs in the sky over the field. The aliens on the ground scrambled to avoid its light. Within seconds, the light enveloped me. Fear overwhelmed me. No words came as the brighter light surrounded me. I thought it might be the mother ship coming to deal with me once and for all.

The beam began a slow spread outward from my position. Many of the demons turned and ran. I looked up and watched the hole in the sky grow wider. Its brightness burned into my retinas and I fell to my knees, then to the ground, and lay flat against the cold grass. That light was different than the one that paralyzed and stole me so many months ago. A new kind of fear filled me in the face of the small display of Holy power. I knew that even that tiny portion of His holiness would kill me if I experienced it directly. I covered my head with my heads and continued singing songs of praise to my God. It felt like an eternity until the wind stopped.

Rise up, Alex. Your enemies have been defeated.

Impossible.

Filled with doubt, I opened my eyes and dared to look at the section of yard straight ahead of me. There were no more greys standing in the field, and no more lights on the horizon. It took several moments for my eyes to adjust to the darkness. The stars that burned bright and the pale light of the moon allowed a little illumination.

I turned my head to look behind me. There was no sign of the UFOs or the greys, only the frosted dead grass and the dirt of the driveway. Tears came hot and heavy. I choked out more praise to God for his obvious display of power. As I pushed myself up off the ground, I was overwhelmed with gratitude for deliverance from my enemies.

But my fight was far from over.

• 22 •

I rose to my feet and noticed an orange glow in the field behind the house. It was followed by another about fifty yards from the first, and I wondered if it was a different type of illusion. By the time I spotted another I knew what it was. Fire.

I jumped to my feet and ran to the back of the house. At least a dozen more fires lined the border of my property on the east, north, and south. There were none to the west, which was where the farm bordered the road. I squinted and thought I saw a shadow running to my left, holding what could have been a torch. The shape paused for a moment and another orange flame erupted from the ground. On my right, another fire was lit. I ran to the front porch and into the house.

Once inside, I rushed to the kitchen, picked up the landline phone I never used and dialed 911. There was nothing but dead air. I pressed the receiver button down to reset the connection. Nothing.

In the best of circumstances, help could arrive

within thirty minutes, maybe fifteen if police, fire, and emergency services were already in the area. Chances of that were pretty slim, considering the sleepy nature of the backcountry and the fact it was the middle of the night. My location was so remote that my property would be beyond saving at least ten to twenty minutes before help arrived. I dropped the house phone and went hunting for my cell phone.

I found it in the bedroom. Dialing 911 proved tricky as my shaking hands and fingers got in the way.

The dispatch operator answered quickly. "911, what's your emergency."

The words flew out of my mouth. "My field is on fire, and I think someone's out there lighting it."

After confirming my address, she assured me help was on the way, and tried to keep me on the phone. I begged her to hurry and ended the call.

I needed to put on some better clothes and find my dog, who'd moved from under the bed. I grabbed a pair of crumpled jeans, a clean but wrinkled long sleeve t-shirt, and a pair of socks. Once I wrangled on the clothes, I shoved my feet into my work boots and ran out of the room calling for Charlie.

I found him in the kitchen, staring into the backyard through the sliding glass door, growling. I looked through the pane of glass and was shocked to see an amorphous black shape the size of a human on the other side. It held a burning torch in one hand. I wondered if it was another kind of demon I had not encountered. I watched as the torch lowered and the flames set the siding on fire. Panic rose in my chest.

Do not be afraid. I am with you.

How could I not be afraid?

I screamed, crouched down, and put my hands

over my head as I heard an explosion from outside. Charlie started barking and ran with me to the front door. I stumbled out onto the porch. The explosion was from the propane tank at the far end of the garage. Fire spread in all directions. I was torn between going back into the house and running away from it.

My decision was made even more difficult as Carla walked toward the porch. She was dressed in all black, except for her shock of blond hair that blew freely in the night breeze. A wild, fervent look on her face was made even more startling by the reflection of the torch in her hand. The flames reflected in her eyes and I cringed at the sight of her. Was this the evil that had hidden behind her seemingly benign exterior all this time?

She stepped forward and faced me as she lowered the torch in her hand to the ground. The fire spread toward the house. I stood my ground and engaged her in conversation to stall for time.

"Why are you doing this to me, Carla?"

She stood up to her full height and glared at me. "You still haven't figured it out yet, Alex. You are a threat to our mission." Spittle flew from her mouth.

"What mission is that? Siccing your demented pets on other people to torture them?"

Charlie growled at her.

"No, stupid. The mission is to get people's eyes off God. And to have a little fun watching morons like you squirm in the process." She threw her head back and cackled like a witch.

I shivered at the sound.

"That still doesn't explain why you're setting my house on fire."

"That's not all we came to do, Alex. You need to be silenced."

257

Something in her eyes darkened, and I knew her murderous intentions for me. With nowhere else to go I ran back into the house and slammed the front door closed behind me. Smoke from near the sliding glass door poured into the living room. I coughed and put my sleeve over my face.

Charlie followed me as I rushed toward the source of the smoke. I felt the heat from the fire as it penetrated the inside of the house. I turned at the kitchen and opened the breezeway door that led to the garage. Charlie raced ahead of me, reading my thoughts. I let him go and looked back into the house for a moment. Everything I had ever known was going up in flames. Part of me wanted to try to save it, but I knew I had to try to save myself first.

I took one last glance at the living room as a Molotov cocktail crashed through the living room window. It hit the coffee table and spurts of yellow fire exploded as the glass bottle shattered. The curtains on the front window burst into hungry flames that climbed to the ceiling. I stepped into the breezeway and started running toward the door to the garage.

The thought that I might be running into a trap crossed my mind, but there was nowhere else I could go. The front and back door were blocked by fire, and this exit wouldn't be far behind. Going back the way I came would be suicide. If I could reach my truck before it was set ablaze I might have a chance to make it out alive.

I held the doorknob in my hand, closed my eyes, and turned it slowly. As I pushed the door open, I realized I'd left my keys on the kitchen table. I cursed myself for my stupidity and sprinted back into the breezeway toward the main part of the house. A black shape stormed past the doorway and I pressed my back to the wall, hoping to hide in the shadows. Something heavy and wooden smashed to the ground inside.

I dared a glance at the opening. I couldn't see anyone from my limited viewpoint. There was no time to wait and the risk was unavoidable. I ran toward the inferno when I should have been running away. The heat inside was oppressive, and the smoke stung my eyes and lungs. I had only taken a few steps inside before I saw my keys on the kitchen table, the dull metal reflecting the orange glow. I snatched them up and retreated to the door.

A step inside the breezeway I sensed a presence behind me. I turned and faced the black shape I'd noticed a moment earlier. It was the tall man I had seen in Carla's home the night she and the others summoned the greys. I took a step back, stumbled over my feet, and fell onto my butt. I knew I was dead. There was nowhere to go and he had all the advantage.

He was on top of me in seconds, holding me down and reaching to his side for what I assumed was a gun, knife, or some other weapon to silence me forever. I squirmed underneath him, but it was no use. He was stronger than he should have been.

Ask and it shall be given to you.

An idea struck me. I became very still and in the softest audible voice possible said, "In the name of Jesus Christ, son of God, I command you to come out of this man."

The reaction was immediate. The tall man released me, scampered away, and started screaming. He held the sides of his head as a black liquid poured out of his mouth and onto the ground like vomit. I scrambled backwards against the wall but stayed close enough to watch.

As soon as the tar-like goo left his body, the tall man became enraged. He ran at me and knocked me to the ground as I tried to stand. I punched and kicked and thrashed, and he did the same. His superhuman strength was gone and I thought there was a chance I could win the fight against him.

I heard the growl and sharp warning bark from Charlie before I knew what was happening. A blinding flash of teeth and fur rushed past my head. A half second later I heard the tall man screaming in pain. He yelled at my dog to let go, but Charlie disobeyed that order. I pushed myself up off the ground and watched as my dog's strong jaws clamped onto the tall man's leg. They both fell back into the steps leading into the kitchen. The man beat at Charlie's head, but my good dog would not let go.

It was enough for the tall man to be maimed and not be able to catch up to me. I whistled and Charlie let go of the man's leg. He snapped his head toward me, spraying a line of blood against the wall. His mouth and muzzle were red and wet. A few fleshy ribbons of gore hung from his teeth. He shook his head, creating a spray of blood, and leapt over to me. I was horrified and proud at the same time. The tall man screamed in agony as the fire raged behind him.

I sprinted into the garage. As I opened the truck door, Charlie jumped in and laid down on the passenger side of the bench seat. He licked his chops and I thought I was going to be sick. Adrenalin overrode my disgust and I climbed in next to him. I sat in the cab for a moment, planning my escape. The tall man was temporarily sidetracked, but I had Carla, Phil, and Ellie to consider, if not more people who wanted to kill me.

I am with you.

That thought gave me the only encouragement I needed. I started the truck engine and pressed the garage door remote at the same time. Both machines rumbled to life. I shifted into reverse and waited for my chance to punch the gas and race toward an uncertain future.

As the garage door slid along its track, I watched Carla come into view through the side mirror. She stood outside the garage with her eyes closed, still as a statue, as though she was not aware that the truck was running and ready to move in her direction. I hesitated, but only for a second.

Carla's eyes snapped open and I knew they were not human. The dark pools revealed her as either demon possessed or a demon herself. It didn't really matter which it was. The garage door was not fully open when I floored the gas pedal. The tires squealed against the cement and the metal garage door scraped against the roof of the truck cab as it rushed backward. There was a sickening thump as I smashed into Carla's body. I kept driving until I was sure she was clear of the tires.

I slammed the brakes and stared at her body laid out in the driveway. She was face up and one leg was bent at an unnatural angle. I felt a twinge of guilt about running her over and contemplated getting out of the truck to make sure she was okay. I got over any feelings of guilt pretty fast.

The bent leg moved into its correct position with a crack and snap that I could hear over the running engine. She rolled over to one side in a single jerking motion and rose to her feet. An ocean of fire raged behind her as she turned to face me. Her eyes were blacker than the darkest night, and there was no mystery about her fury. She took a step toward me and fell as she, or more accurately the creature within her, tried to put weight on the broken leg. She let out a shriek of surprise, followed by a cackle reserved for the insane.

Instead of waiting around, I let my foot off the brake and punched the gas. Halfway down the driveway, I jerked the wheel and slid into a forward facing position. Dust swirled around me. My heart pounded so fast and my thinking was so irrational, I'm surprised I had the presence of mind to depress the clutch, shift slowly into first and press lightly on the gas to prevent the engine from stalling.

I didn't bother looking back at the house once the truck hit the pavement. I just turned left and headed toward Avondale. About a mile down the road I heard the first sirens blaring nearby, and pulled over to the shoulder. My first thought was to bow my head and pray. The shaking in my hands prevented me from clasping them together as I prayed.

When I opened my eyes, the lights of two SUV's owned by the Forest County Sheriff's Department crested a hill, followed by a fire truck and EMS. They raced past me, lights blazing and sirens blaring. I knew I should go back, but part of me wanted more than anything to just take off down the open road and never look return.

Instead, I made a u-turn and headed back to the farm. There was no question that nothing would be left to save. Aside from the numbness of being in shock, there was no sense of mourning as the home I'd lived in my whole life burned to ashes.

An orange glow in the sky as I drove closer told me all I needed to know. Once I passed the tree line at the edge of the property, I saw the house fully engulfed in flames. Something exploded inside, creating a fireball that blew off part of the roof. Smoke and flames poured out of the main house, breezeway, garage and the field beyond it. Nothing was spared.

I pulled into the driveway, rolled down my window, and stayed far back from the flashing lights. A happy memory of my family eating a traditional Thanksgiving dinner cracked through a wall in my brain and emotion overwhelmed me. Just a minute before I couldn't wait to leave it all behind and then nostalgia appeared from nowhere. I thought of my mother's bible that I'd never found, and many other little things that reminded me of our lives in that place.

I scanned the yard for any sign of Carla, Phil, Ellie, or the tall man, but there was none. My assumption was that they scattered at the sound of sirens. The presence of law enforcement was probably a big deterrent to a group of murderers.

Charlie put his paws on the dashboard and watched as the only home he had ever known was destroyed. He let out one whimper, turned toward me and panted a few times before laying back down on the seat.

The fire department never bothered trying to save the house. Their primary concern was making sure the fire did not spread to the neighbors. I sat and watched the odd beauty of the destructive power with a strange mix of emotions. The roof caved in and a shower of sparks billowed into the sky. I sucked in a breath through my teeth.

Breaking the curse that plagued me was the end of one part of my life and the beginning of another. There was nothing but a blank slate ahead of me. It was strange to feel a sense of hope while watching my former life turn to ashes. I thanked God for rescuing me so many times I'd lost count. My future was uncertain, but I had Him, my dog, and my crappy old truck.

• 23 •

The next day I discovered Carla and her strange crew never left the property. Their burned bodies were found just inside the front door. I wondered about the motivation for such drastic action. Either they were all crazy, or the entities they worshipped forced them to destroy themselves. It was horrible to contemplate the fate that awaited them on the other side of this world. Despite her betrayal, that wild-haired woman had set me on a path to the truth.

I stayed with Alicia and her family while I decided what to do next. She loved hearing me tell the story of my harrowing escape. Seeing the way she interacted with her husband and children had me thinking about starting my own family someday. I knew if that happened it was still a long way off.

A few days after the fire, I reached out to Ron Lincoln to fill him in on how everything shook out. He was so impressed that he begged me to join him as his assistant. He promised low pay, a lot of travel, and bottom of the barrel lodging and food, but it was an opportunity to restart. A couple of weeks later, I turned in my resignation at Avondale farms.

I kept the property in my name but leased it out to neighbors who'd make it a proper farm. The house was paid off, and I used the insurance settlement to demolish the house and garage, which made a nice flat piece of land to grow corn, soybeans, or whatever else the land could produce. I never once regretted my decision not to rebuild.

● ● ●

After about two months on the road with Ron Lincoln, I was getting the hang of the festival circuit. While he focused on the presentation and delivery of his message, I was responsible for providing my own testimony and administrative work. I booked the venues, hotel rooms, and provided anything else we might need with next to no money. The provision was miraculous and I learned to lean a lot on God and not on my own understanding. There was nothing quite like being one step away from destitution to keep a person focused on faith.

During a festival in some far-flung town in the Arizona desert, we were visited by an interesting man. He arrived early and sat in the back, silent and unassuming. His gaze never wavered from the stage, and he smiled as I gave my testimony at the end of Ron's speech.

When the presentation ended, the few people who sat through the entire thing wandered out, but he remained. I tried to study him without being obvious. Each time I glanced over his eyes locked on mine and I turned away. His interest was unsettling.

Under my breath, I said, "Ron, do you see that guy back there. Don't look!"

Ron nodded his head. "I've seen him before. He'll wait a minute before approaching us." Ron looked me in the eye. "It's important for you to listen to what he has to say. It could be crucial to your future, our future."

The fact that Ron knew him gave me some assurance that the borderline creep was not a complete stranger. I wondered what he had to share with me. It was sure to have something to do with the supernatural. Instead of dwelling on it, I started packing up the handouts, business cards, and flyers that were part of the presentation.

A soft, strong voice that came from behind startled me. "Alex, it's a pleasure to meet you. My name is Lucas Stone. But please call me Luke."

I turned around, expecting to see a person standing at or above my eye level. I was surprised to look down to see the man from the back of the room seated in a wheelchair. He offered me a smile that held some hidden knowledge. I reached out and shook his hand.

He gave me a little smirk. "How much has Ron told you about me, Alex?"

"Very little I must admit. Just that what you have to say may be of particular interest to me."

Luke shifted in his wheelchair. "I have had my share of experiences with the supernatural, to say the least. I've also known the kind of life those without hope experience. And I've been up close and personal with a demon-possessed man."

I gulped. My own experience with aliens and

demons was more than enough for one lifetime.

"Our enemy is crafty, Alex. I have long felt that something big is coming and people like you and me are part of a plan to expose the lies and tell as many people as possible the truth. Your work here with Ron is proof that you are committed to that mission as well."

I had no idea what he meant by something big.

"I believe that a time is coming when much of the Christian world will vanish in the blink of an eye, and the most plausible explanation will be alien abduction. Your experience and countless others are part of a vast plan to drive people further away from the Word of God during the time when they should be turning to Him the most."

A strange feeling settled onto the back of my neck and traveled down my spine. What he said resonated as the truth. That was why Carla, or the demon within her, was so driven to destroy me. She knew I would expose the truth for as long as I had breath to whoever would listen. She paid for her failure with her life in this world and the next.

"Thank you for the encouragement. I'll do my best to expose the truth where I can. It was nice to meet you. Will I see you again?"

Luke smiled. "Oh, yes. I have a feeling we will see each other again."

He shook my hand and rolled away in the wheelchair. He stopped and talked to Ron for a few minutes while I finished packing up. I had the feeling they were talking about me.

After Luke left, Ron approached me and smiled. "Thank you for meeting with Lucas, Alex. I think it encourages him that there are still some people left willing to embrace the light and shun the darkness. We need all the help we can get in these dark days."

It struck me that Ron called him Lucas. I assumed it was a formality, a quirk of Ron's personality.

I almost turned my back on him to continue cleaning up but didn't. "Luke said something about what happened to me being a part of something bigger. He did talk about the rapture of Christians, but I had the feeling it wasn't that. Do you know what he meant?"

Ron smiled. "You are a very perceptive young man, Alex. Lucas and I have known for some time that the demons are preparing for their false messiah to take power and deceive the whole world. They have done everything they can to turn the tide of humanity against God. And to some extent, they have succeeded. But as long as there are people like you, me, and Lucas around, they will never be able to truly take hold of the power they crave."

I nodded, feeling both important and small at the same time. My hope was that just sharing my own experience could inspire hope in others. Maybe I should have felt a great weight of responsibility for delivering the truth to the masses, but my heart was light.

"I guess we better get to work then."

● ● ●

My life was changed by my experience with the paranormal. It would be a lie to say that I never felt the icy tendrils of fear again, or that there were no times I just wanted to give up. I spent many sleepless nights in a cold sweat, afraid of things I had seen.

The biggest lesson I learned was to not take anything for granted. For too long I lived my life like a zombie, existing without any real purpose. Once I discovered the truth, everything changed and each day became a new opportunity to explore what it means to be truly alive.

CHECK OUT THESE OTHER THRILLING TITLES FROM JESS HANNA:

www.ingramcontent.com/pod-product-compliance
Lightning Source LLC
Chambersburg PA
CBHW052038240626
47153CB00006B/2146